BITTER

BITTER

VICK BREEDY

DEDICATION

I dedicate this book to my son. I didn't know what love was until God blessed me with you.

ACKNOWLEDGEMENTS

I thank you God for giving me the courage to complete this book. Thank you to my family and friends that took moments out of their lives to bring this book to life. I am forever grateful.

CONTENTS

BITTER BEGINNINGS

Ava:

I asked her who my dad was. She said "some weak motherfucker." When I asked her if he had a name, she smacked the shit out of me. I never met my dad. The only information that I had to go on, I learned from overhearing my mom on a telephone call with him.

"Oh, so you were ok with my black skin when you were dipping your married pink penis in and out of me for damn near a decade . . .No! You listen!"

That was all I heard. She went into her bedroom, closed the door and turned on the music so that I couldn't eavesdrop. The bitch never said his name. With minimal information to go on, the conversation revealed that my dad was white and already had a wife.

Every time I did something wrong, this bitch would say that I was just like my weak ass daddy. The older I got, the more she thought I looked like him. I figured it must be true, because I didn't resemble her in any way.

I am built like my mom, but I look nothing like her. Her skin is chocolate and mine isn't. Her hair is dark and coarse; I have light brown and silky hair. Her eyes are the color of coal and mine are caramel brown.

Many people consider me to be beautiful. I have a black woman's body and the features of a white woman. My mom would never believe it, but I grew up wishing that I looked more like her. I felt alienated by her and even worse, I felt as she hated me. I am my mom's only child.

I needed her love, but all I got was her bitterness. She made me pay for the crimes of a father that I never knew.

In high school, I always had boys that wanted to get with me. Of course, that was the reasons the sisters at school couldn't stand me. I was the girl that they were referring to when you heard, "She thinks she's cute." It actually hurt my feelings that most of the black females didn't like me, just because of my looks.

Based on how I acted, however, they never knew my true feelings. I gave the girls at the Burke exactly who they wanted. They thought that I was stuck up and I played the part. It was easier than showing them my insecurities. I was more insecure in my beauty than they ever could have imagined.

Black women just didn't like me. My own black mother couldn't stand me. The girls at school were no exception. Most kids grow up knowing that their parents love them, whereas I grew up knowing that my mother hated me. It had nothing to do with how I behaved at home or school; instead, it had everything to do with who my father was. I hated him for leaving me with his mistress.

Charlene:

Monday through Friday, I spent at my mom's house. Weekends and summers, my time was spent at my dad's house. My parents got divorced while I was in junior high. Every time I was at my dad's house, he'd drill me for information about my mom. She did the same thing whenever I was with him; it was sickening.

I usually got whatever I asked for. If Mom said no, I'd go to Dad and he'd say yes. Birthdays and Christmas time were like competitions to see who could spend the most on Charlene. As a teenager, that was one of the many benefits of having divorced parents.

There were also many disadvantages. I had to choose which side of the family's outings that I would go to. I never spent weekends with my mom and my dad often worked weekends. On those weekends that my dad had to work, I wound up spending time with my paternal grandmother. I didn't like being around her, because all she did was chain-smoke and talk shit about my maternal side of the family.

My friends from school didn't get a chance to hang out with me in the summer or on weekends, because my dad lived so far away from my mom. Nobody was willing to travel, so, I made new ones; I had weekend friends and weekday friends.

I split myself into two different people. When I was at my dad's, I had no rules. Therefore, as "Weekend Charlene", I could have a more carefree attitude with my weekend friends. During the week, when I was home with my mother, "Weekday Charlene" had plenty of rules. I acted more reserved around my weekday friends. I knew that if I got into trouble or embarrassed my mother in any way, there would be hell to pay, because my mother didn't play.

I became friends with a new girl at my school. Her name was Ava. Ava was a weekday friend, but was willing to visit me during the weekend on occasions. This friendship forced me to become one person; I somehow had to merge Weekday Charlene with Weekend

Charlene. It was hard to do, because they were both extreme opposites. I ended up playing it safe and became more of who my mother expected me to be. I shied away from Weekend Charlene; she remained dormant, and only later, would she surface.

Ava and I eventually became best friends. We told each other everything. We were like sisters; we were so tight. Ava and I were the same age, but she acted more like the big sister. She was very protective and very mature. I witnessed her protective nature when we were at North Shore Mall near my father's house.

Ava said that she would go to the store with me. I was dying to buy some shoes that were only in stock at this particular mall. As luck would have it, one of my old weekend friends was working at the shoe store. I was forced to either interact with her or leave without my shoes; leaving shoeless was not an option for me.

When I got to the register, I sheepishly said, "Hi," and handed her my money to pay for the shoes. She wouldn't take the money from my hand and said that I could place it on the counter. Ava didn't like the vibe that she was getting from this girl. Next thing you know, big sis started telling my weekend friend how unprofessional she was. She then threatened her. She encouraged her to value her life and adjust her attitude. My ex weekend friend looked Ava up and down and told her to mind her business, before she called security to say that she felt threatened. Before Ava could go off on her, I intervened.

I knew what the problem was. The last time I spoke to Evelyn, I was supposed to go to a family cookout with her. I ended up not going and never called to explain why. The truth was that I just hadn't felt like going. I was hanging out with Ava so much that I shut other folks out. I kept telling myself that I was going to call her and apologize, but time kept getting away from me and a few days turned into a few months. By then, I was too embarrassed to call her, so I avoided her.

It wasn't anything in particular she did; it was all on me. I explained this to Ava, asked

Evelyn to accept my apology, and I invited her to lunch that day. She said that she had to work a double, but she accepted my apology. Since then, the three of us have been the best of friends. Ava and Evelyn hit it off even better than I expected.

Evelyn:

I'm so tired of his shit! Why won't she just pack our things and leave in the middle of the night like they do on the Lifetime Channel? We can go live in a domestic violence shelter. It has to be better than being a grown woman and getting your ass beat on the regular. If she doesn't do something soon, I will. I've asked her multiple times why she stays with Daddy. He doesn't appreciate her; he walks all over her, literally and figuratively.

She says she married Daddy for good times and bad. I told her that it seems like she's gotten more bad times than good. I wondered just how long she would wait for the good times to get here. Mom doesn't work; she used to before she met Daddy. When they got married, he made her quit her job; he makes plenty money, so she really didn't have to work.

Actually, he makes a lot of money. We have a beautiful home located in Marblehead, with a maid, and a cook; when I was younger, we also had a nanny. I attend private school and want for nothing. The one thing that I did want, the only thing I continually wish for, I never got. She just wouldn't leave my dad.

My mother has skills; it's not as if she wouldn't be able to find a job if she left him. So what; we might not get to live in a huge house with a nice luxury car and have fancy clothes. Her safety and my emotional well-being should be far more valuable to her than wealth.

I couldn't wait to get to college. Watching my father abuse my mother was just too much for me to witness. I kept these beatings a secret, until I became best friends with Charlene and

Ava. I confessed the beatings to them, and also told them my deepest, dirtiest secrets. They had my back and always supported me in whatever I was involved in, whether it was good or bad. Since my mom wouldn't take a stand, I felt that it was my duty to do so.

Ava has plenty of cousins. One of her cousins agreed to help me out for a fee; he said that he would take care of my father for me. He'd hurt him so badly that my dad wouldn't have the strength to raise his hand to my mother. I asked Ava's cousin, Craig, how much this would cost me. I thought that he was going to ask me for a large sum of money, especially since he knew that I had access to it. He surprised me and asked for pussy instead. Craig admitted that he'd wanted to taste me since freshman year. I agreed to his sexual terms and I let him eat me out. I lied to Ava and Charlene, telling them that I gave Craig a few hundred and told him to do what he had to do.

I didn't know what he planned on doing to my dad, but Ava assured me that he would follow through. Craig was gaining a reputation as being someone you didn't want to cross. A week later, I come home from school and my mom is crying as if somebody died. I secretly hoped that someone had died—my dad. Our life would be so much more peaceful if my dad would just keel over and die.

My mom told me that my dad was in the hospital. Somebody ran a red light while he was on his way to work, and crashed into his driver side door. His legs were damn near mangled and the physician didn't know if he was going to be able to walk again. I had no tears nor was there a hint of sadness. Instead, I felt a sense of relief wash over me.

Mom instructed me to get whatever homework I had to complete and grab something to eat, because she and I would be spending the rest of the day at the hospital to be with my father. *Not me, she must be crazy if she thinks I'm going to sit there and act as if I give a damn about someone who doesn't give a damn about her or me.*

11

I ignored her and proceeded to the refrigerator, grabbed something to eat and then went to my room. I wasn't spending my night at the bedside of a man that beat the one person I loved the most. If she had any sense, she'd take this opportunity to leave him. Instead, she assumed the role of the faithful, loyal, supportive wife and spent her nights at the hospital until he was able to return home. How could somebody so smart be so stupid?

I never went to the hospital to visit him. My mom asked me why I refused to go visit my father, and in turn, I asked her why she married my father. She told me that he wasn't always that way. Before they got married, he was a gentler man; it wasn't until after they got married that he started abusing her. After hearing that, I made it up in my mind that I'd never get married. If you couldn't trust that the person you dated would be the same person once you married them, then marriage wasn't for me.

Ava:

I tried out for the basketball team and landed a sixth man spot. I'd never played organized basketball, but decided to give it a try. I played basketball with the boys in my neighborhood for years, so I figured playing with a bunch of girls would be a breeze. I soon found out that it was an entirely different world playing with girls. These bitches were crybabies; all they did was whine and complain about everything. They were weak too; they couldn't do push-ups, half of them couldn't do a pull up, they had no handle and couldn't make a lay-up to save their lives.

I couldn't figure out why I had only earned the sixth man spot. At the half-time mark of our first game, we were losing by twenty points. Unheard of! If that wasn't bad enough, the coach had yet to put me in. I sat next to the assistant coach, trying to ear hustle as usual. I was listening to their strategy and it sounded like a long stretch. When they were done, I got the head coach's attention and told him that not only could I win this game by making lay-ups, I could guarantee that we would beat them by at least ten points. I finally convinced the head coach that he had nothing to lose, because we were down by an embarrassing twenty points already.

Not only did we win by twelve points, I damn near dunked the last shot! Coach is definitely going to have to rethink and restructure the starting roster. Shit! If I didn't mind the responsibility, I'd demand the captain's spot too. If that wasn't an example of leadership, I don't know what is! The girls on the team never gave me dap for winning the game for them; they actually hated on me, every last one of those bitches.

They were mad for all types of reasons. They were mad because my hair didn't nap up when I sweated. They were mad because I still looked like a girl in my basketball uniform, while they looked like middle school boys; I had a voluptuous, yet athletic physique. Most of all, they were mad because all of the boys on the boys' team sweated me, including some of their boyfriends.

Here I was, at a new school and still getting the same shit from bitches! Thank God, Charlene was my friend. If it wasn't for her, I'd be friendless at school. I was actually happy when my mom said that we were moving to this neighborhood, because she needed a new start. I thought to myself that she wasn't the only one that needed a new start. Unfortunately, it was the same shit, different setting.

Christmas was one week away. I had some money saved from my summer job. I went out and bought four presents. The first present I bought was for my mother, a new Coach bag. The second and third gift that I bought was for Charlene and Evelyn. I got them each a Coach wristlet. The last gift that I bought was for me. I went to the local jewelry store and purchased a diamond pendant. I treated myself like I wanted to be treated. If I didn't do it, nobody else would.

On Christmas Day, my mom spent the morning with me, but then she told me at the last minute that she had plans to go out of state with her girlfriend, Rochelle. She would be back on the following Monday. I was pissed, but at the same time, I was okay with this. All she would have done was sit around and complain about how she deserved so much and got so little, when it came to the luxuries life had to offer.

I really don't know how she had any girlfriends. If anyone was doing better than she was, she couldn't handle it. All she did was hate on them. It was kind of like the girls from school; my mother was just an adult version of them. Rochelle, was a straight up hoe. I know this, because I used to sit up at night and listen to her, while she visited my mom. They would drink wine, play cards, and gossip until the middle of the night. I remember one conversation vividly.

"Rochelle, you are a hot mess! I can't believe you messed with that girl's husband."

"Well, this is how I see it. If she was handling her business, the way I do, someone like me wouldn't have had the chance to mess with her husband."

"You are soooooo wrong! God is going to strike you down for thinking like that."

"Bitch, you should talk. You daughter is the product of a broken marriage. Might I remind you that you are the reason why their marriage is broken?"

"Bitch nothing; he and I were together before he married her. That means she's at fault for messing up our relationship, not the other way around."

"Hoe, you must forget who you are talking to. I was with you that night at the sex club. He was drunk and you were high. I remember him telling you he was engaged to be married, but once you gave him that serious head game, he forgot all about his fiancée. I must admit, I learned a thing or two from you, but you messed up when you spit his stuff out. If you swallowed like I do, you could get a man to do damn near anything for you."

"I ain't swallowing that poison!"

"Listen and learn. When I need a bill paid, I swallow. When I need a vacation, I swallow. When I need a new outfit, I swallow and when I want a new car, I take it up the butt!"

After that comment, I remember my mother laughing so hard that she snorted. I also learned that the key to a man's heart isn't through his tummy. That conversation shaped who I became sexually. I learned that Rochelle was right and my mother had a lot to learn.

Years later, Rochelle is the same hoe she was before. My mom better watch her back with Rochelle; she may think Rochelle's her girl, but Rochelle is selfish. If it comes down to her choosing between my mom's friendship and a man, the man will win every time. I just hope my mom understands that about her.

Evelyn:

Its Christmas time and I'm depressed. My mom is waiting on my father hand and foot. I mistakenly thought that since he couldn't walk anymore, he couldn't terrorize my mother. Instead of physically abusing her, now he just does it verbally. He talks so much trash that I just want someone to punch him in his mouth.

I didn't feel the slightest bit of guilt for arranging for him to get hurt. He didn't talk to me and I didn't talk to him. We both acted as if we didn't exist in each other's world. I'd come into the house and walk right by him without saying hello. He was no better. My father would roll himself into the living room and change the channel that I was watching, as if I wasn't watching it. He paid the bills, so I really couldn't complain.

I didn't expect anything from him for Christmas and I didn't bother to get him a present either. My mother got us presents from each other. She couldn't stand that my father and I no longer talked. She was such a peacemaker, but there would be no truce as long as I was living under that roof. Next year, I'd be going to college and I couldn't wait to get away from this dysfunction!

Craig came over and spent the night with me Christmas night and I let him do more than taste me; I let him enter me. My mom never checked on me after 8 pm, because my father required her to be on duty from 8 pm until the next morning. She didn't bother me and I didn't bother her. The last thing I'd want to see is her riding my father in his wheelchair.

Once I lost my virginity to Craig, he slept over many nights after that. I don't know if my mom knew, or if she just didn't care. I never told Charlene or Ava about my lust-filled late nights with Craig; I knew that Craig wouldn't tell them either. We weren't boyfriend and girlfriend; we just had a sexual arrangement, and that made it bearable for me to get through my last year living in my father's home.

If Craig had gone to college, he would be a sophomore right now. I asked him if he thought about going to college and he said that the streets were his key to higher learning, so we never discussed school again. Craig was making a name for himself in Mission Hill, but it was a life that I wanted nothing to do with. Craig was my stress reliever and that's it; nothing more, and nothing less.

Don't get me wrong; Craig is fine. He looks like a young LL Cool J. He has a confident walk, an infectious smile and a big dick. I may not have been with anyone other than Craig, but I've definitely seen my fair share of dicks. Craig has a porno dick, the kind that should be on film for the entire world to admire.

I plan on going to an out of state college. If not out of state, somewhere far enough to feel like I'm out of state. I hope that Ava and Charlene will be going too. Once I get into school that will be the end of my good dick arrangement; Craig will be missed.

Charlene:

Christmastime looked like I'd hit the lottery. I got doubles of everything; some of my gifts I ended up giving to Evelyn and Ava. My parents didn't really communicate with me; they just asked what I wanted for Christmas and I told them both the same exact thing.

I figured if one parent didn't get it, the other one would. I never thought both of them would actually get me everything that I asked for. I didn't have the heart to tell them that they'd gotten me the same thing, so I just acted extremely grateful to make them feel good.

My boyfriend came over to give me my gift. I really didn't know what to expect; we just started dating three months ago and we hadn't exchanged gifts before. I went out and got him a designer watch from Macy's. He gave me a gift bag from the dollar store, filled with four mini lip-glosses.

Of course, I acted grateful; I'm really good at that. I would have preferred that he got me a Hallmark card instead. This fool didn't even buy the lip-glosses. In small print, they said not for resale. They were gifts that you get for free when you purchased a more expensive item. I later learned that his other girlfriend got the real gift and he gave me the freebies; needless to say, we broke up before the New Year.

The next boyfriend I had was no better. He didn't cheat on me, at least not that I know of. He was just a pervert. All he wanted to do is try freaky things with me. Now I was no virgin, but by no means was I a freak. We broke up the night he asked me to let him stick a banana up my vagina. The crazy thing is, he wasn't the worst boyfriend I had during my senior year.

The worst was this guy that asked me to sit on his face. I was all for it until he asked me to fart while I was sitting there! After that one, I decided to give dating a break until I started college. Where were all of the normal guys?

It was Valentine's Day and I was boyfriend-less. I was okay with that though. My track record with men hadn't been the most fulfilling. Ava and Evelyn didn't have a date that night either, so, we decided to all meet up and have a girl's night in. We all stayed over at Ava's house. Her mom was out on a date, so we had the house to ourselves. We played Truth or Dare, ate junk food and shared a bottle of wine.

We learned a lot about each other that night. We also learned about a side of Ava that we didn't know existed. Ava had some anger that she was suppressing. She had a love/hate relationship with her mom. I knew that it would be a matter of time before she went off on her mom, and I was concerned. I told her that whenever she needed to talk about her feelings, she should call me. I didn't want her to make herself sick harboring so much anger. She promised me that she would call me and she did.

A few weeks later, Ava called me at midnight and she was crying hysterically. When she finally calmed down enough for me to find out what happened, I couldn't believe my ears. Ava told me that her mom was drunk and she was talking crap about how Ava pranced around like she was "the flyest bitch around"; her words, not mine. Rochelle was over at the house too, drinking and cosigning everything that Ava's mom said.

By the end of the story, they'd cut Ava's hair off and she'd stabbed Rochelle with the same scissors. Ava said that if her mother hadn't run out of the house, she would have stabbed her too. She spent the night at my house that night. Rochelle lived, but Ava's relationship with her mom was severed. I helped Ava cut the rest of her hair off so that it looked as if the cut was intentional. Ava was even more beautiful with her hair short. Her mom's attempt at making her ugly failed.

The next day was a school day, but I told Ava that she should skip school and take a mental health day. Ava didn't want her mom to know that she had shaken her up. Ava told me that she wasn't going to give that bitch the satisfaction. She got up, got dressed, and went to school.

As expected, she got plenty of stares. The females still shot her disapproving looks, but it was only because they were jealous that they wouldn't look half as good as Ava did, if they cut their hair or took their weaves out. The dudes at school were salivating when she walked by. Ava said that since her hair was short like a boy's, she had to play up all of her other womanly attributes to compensate for the lack of hair. I told her that there was no need. Anyone with eyes could see that Ava was all woman; no ifs, ands, or buts about that.

Ava contemplated getting a tattoo just to spite her mother. She settled on getting a t-shirt made that read, "THE FLYEST BITCH AROUND" in big exaggerated gold letters. The T-shirt was white and it fit her like it was spandex. She got sent home from school as soon as one of the teachers realized what the shirt said. The next day she came to school with a shirt that was made the exact same way, except it was red with exaggerated big white letters that read, "YOU WANNA BE ME."

If Ava thought that she had haters before, they multiplied by one thousand after she wore those shirts. The funny thing is that she is right; she is fly and girls want to look like her. I know that she did it out of spite for her mother and other haters, but the truth really hurt the girls' ego at our school. I was Ava's only friend, besides Evelyn and it remained that way until the day that we graduated.

Ava:

That BITCH, Rochelle cut my hair off! Once I realized what she had done, it was on! During the ambush, I was able to grab the scissors out of her hand. Once I did, I instinctively stabbed her. Her nasty blood squirted directly onto my cheek, just missing my eye. Normally, I wouldn't have done something as life-threatening as stabbing someone, but I just lost it. All of the self-control I had disappeared. I was in a fit of rage at that moment; I even contemplated stabbing my mother too.

After this happened, I called Charlene, who immediately came to the rescue. She has no idea how outside of my mind I was that night. Had she known, she wouldn't have or shouldn't have allowed me to spend the night. I was plotting all types of murderous activities that night to do to my mother. She needed to be punished for letting her hoe-ass friend do that to me. My mom actually held me down and laughed the entire time Rochelle chopped away at my hair; that shit wasn't funny.

That night, my constant yearning for my mom's approval, love and affection came to a complete halt. She became my enemy. As soon as I left for college; I acted as if she was dead. I never called her and I never went home for breaks.

When I got out of school, I never told her that I graduated. That piece of shit never called to check on me, either. After all, she was the mother. She was supposed to care about the well-being of her daughter. Oh well, fuck that bitch. She knew she was wrong! Evelyn, Charlene and I all applied to and got accepted to the same schools. We couldn't figure out which one to go to, until our financial aid package made the decision for us. We all ended up going to UMASS Amherst. It wasn't out of state, but it was far away enough to feel like we were out of state.

College was a whole lot better for me than high school. In college, I got the chance to embrace my beauty instead of being ashamed of it. I wasn't hated on for it. There were many beautiful women in college, so in this atmosphere, I was able to blend in.

Don't get me wrong, I was still one of the most beautiful women on campus. Since there were so many women from every ethnicity that you could think of, I became one of many. This was fine with me, because it allowed me to blend in with the crowd.

I was not a virgin by the time I got to college. I had not been with a lot of men, but enough to where I felt I was experienced. In college there weren't just male students, but there were older men. There were professors. I got involved with one of my professors and he turned me out.

By my senior year, I knew that I could star in an adult film, but I kept all of this a secret from my girls. I had boyfriends throughout college, but none of them could keep me satisfied like the professor I was sleeping with. I realized I had to stop seeing him when I started comparing every guy I met to him.

I knew that he was too old for me to consider having a serious relationship with. He was good in bed and kept my bank account with a substantial cushion, but he just wasn't boyfriend material. This man spoiled me and that made it hard for me to take guys my age seriously.

None of them could measure up or quench my sexual appetite. I soon gave up on trying to get someone that could make me feel as good as the professor. I decided I needed someone normal as a companion, someone that wanted me as a wife. He didn't need to lace my pockets like the professor or blow my back out; he just needed to love me for me. I wanted the love that I never got from my parents.

After I graduated, I moved back to Lynn, Massachusetts. There was no way that I was going to voluntarily live in Amherst. Outside of the campus, it wasn't diverse enough for me. I needed to be around lots of different people. I needed to reside in a city that had a variety of ethnicities, a melting pot atmosphere.

I asked my cousin, Craig, to meet me at a local sub shop not far from my apartment. He had been away for a week in Rhode Island. I wanted to know what he was up to and why he stayed a week in Rhode Island. I got to the sub shop before him and secured a booth next to the window. I was able to see Craig jump out of his Jason Statham Audi as if he was *The Transporter*.

As soon as he sat down, I asked him why he was in Rhode Island for so long. He nonchalantly said his main girl got arrested and he had to figure a few things out and rearrange a few other things. I asked him why he didn't bail her out. He mentioned that I asked too many questions.

Craig then told me that she'd been arrested for something not associated with what she does for him. He left it at that and so did I. Craig was into lots of different things. He is a real hustler; good at everything he involves himself in. His mother has a great business mind too; come to think of it, a lot of us in the family have a great knack for business, but none of us use it for legal purposes.

As much as I hate to admit it, my mother has a superior business mind. Some of it rubbed off on me. I planned on getting a master's degree in business. I will be the first one in the family to actually put my business acumen to good use.

As Craig and I leave the sub shop, I noticed that the guy that made our subs digging in his ear and then going right back to handling the food. I was so grossed out by that. I was gonna tell Craig, but then I decided against it. There's no telling what Craig would do to him. I just acted like it never happened. Shortly after that incident, SARS was on the rise. I gave up Chinese food for two years. It may sound stupid, but I was paranoid.

Craig and I left the sub shop and he drove me back to my apartment. On the way there, we talked about me no longer being his connect at school. He asked me to reconsider, but I told him that I was done with that. It was good while I was in undergrad, but it was getting old. If he had another hustle for me on a larger scale, then I was with it. If not, I told him to count me out.

I still remember that night he drove me to my dorm. My hoopty had broken down and I didn't have AAA. During the ride back to the campus, he asked me a lot of questions about the girls living in my dorm. He wanted to know who had boyfriends, who had low self-esteem, who were gold diggers and who were lesbians. I asked Craig if he was looking for a girlfriend or something and he laughed at me as if I was crazy. He told me that he doesn't deal with young bitches like that; he'd rather deal with the older ones.

Craig asked me if I wanted to do some of his recruiting and he'd pay me a finder's fee for each one that decided to work for him. I really didn't want to get involve with drugs, I needed to know what kind of work he was talking about. So, I made him spell it out for me. Craig was talking about pimping. We went over the details and I quickly figured out that I was definitely something that I thought that I could do. In the end, he agreed to give me $500 for each successful referral. He originally said $250, but I know my worth. He'd make $500 off them in no time.

At the end of my senior year, I stopped recruiting. By then I'd upped my price to $1000 for each girl and I arranged to get another $500 if they were still working by their six-month mark. I'd saved a lot of cash by graduation; I was always good at saving money. Having a steady income was necessary for me.

Between the professor and Craig, I had some serious loot saved. When I left school, I no longer had either income. I'd stopped dealing with the Professor. Craig didn't have anything that I'd do that was worth the risk. I knew now that I had to get a regular job. I didn't want any questions from anyone; having too much cash on hand and no job could cause unnecessary and unwanted attention.

As close as I was to the girls, I always kept my questionable activities to myself. They knew nothing about my dealings with the professor or Craig; I knew about Craig and Evelyn, but I never told her that I knew. I didn't want them in my business, so I never brought up their business. Miss "Goody Two Shoes Charlene" had some skeletons in her closet that she thought nobody knew about.

Overall, college was a good experience for me. It gave me the independence that I needed. I was free from my mother's emotional abuse and that alone did wonders for me. My self-esteem increased greatly; I learned to love myself. I was no longer ashamed of my beauty. I learned how to use my beauty and gift of gab to my advantage. My hair had grown back and my body was even tighter than it was in high school. A high-protein diet and four days at the gym a week did wonders for my body.

Charlene:

College was a blur; I had many fun nights with the girls and I had tried a few drugs just to say that I tried them. I did a few things just to say that I did it once. Some things I told my crew and some things I left out. I knew that they were new to "Weekend Charlene" and I didn't want them to judge me; I wanted to live life with little to no restrictions.

My mom had kept me sheltered, and once I got to school, I went a little crazy. In one weekend, I had a series of threesomes. One night I had sex with two women at the same time. The next night I had sex with two men. On the third night, I had sex with a married couple. I wanted to try everything; my motto became, "I couldn't knock it until I tried it."

I had a few steady boyfriends, but the relationships never lasted. Being so far away from home enabled me to rekindle my friendship with "Weekend Charlene;" I missed her. Ava and

Evelyn thought that I lost my mind when my behavior went from one extreme to the next; there was no middle of the road with me. They were accustomed to dealing with "Weekday Charlene" throughout our friendship.

By senior year, I'd settled down and tried to become "Weekday Charlene" again. It was time to enter the real world; all of my experimentation needed to come to an end. Things had gotten a little out of hand and it took me reaching out to Craig to get things back under control.

I voluntarily let the starting five on the basketball team run a train on me, but I had no idea that someone had planted a camera in the room. I did all types of freaky things. One by one, I let them eat me out front and back. I then returned the favor and gave them all head. I don't know if it was the alcohol or not, but I became ambitious and tried to give two of them head at the same time; I actually tried to stuff two dicks in my mouth!

Things were getting too freaky for my liking; I wanted to stop and they didn't. I pleaded with them to let me go, but they weren't hearing it. They started calling me a whore, telling me that I knew I liked it rough. I was afraid and crying, but they didn't care; they were too busy laughing.

Thirty minutes later felt like three hours later. I was raw, swollen and confused. They told me that they filmed me. They even showed me the film. They conveniently stopped filming right at the part when I changed my mind. These guys threatened to put the video on the internet if I even thought about going to the police.

With that video, I knew that nobody would believe that they raped me, because I looked like a willing participant; I actually looked like the aggressor. I was so embarrassed and angry at myself for getting myself into that predicament. After that night, I vowed to bury "Weekend Charlene" and leave her there, never to be dug up again.

Craig made sure that they never came around me again; he threatened their lives if the video ever made its way to the internet. Anybody that knew Craig or had heard about him, knew enough not to want to get on his bad side. Thankfully, the video never got out. That incident really changed my whole outlook on sex and experimentation. It was a hard lesson to learn, but one I took to heart. I was so shaken up by it that I vowed to never give head again.

Evelyn:

College was more business than pleasure for me. I was determined to excel; I didn't want to have to rely on my father's wealth to live a good life. I made sure that I secured my future by getting a great education. Don't get me wrong; I went to parties here and there with the girls. I made time for fun, but books came first.

I made sure that I had at least a part-time job throughout the semester and worked full-time hours during the summers. I couldn't imagine living a life dependent on a man like my mom had; I'd rather die than live the life she lived. She is still married to my father and still takes his shit.

Every time I checked in with her during the schoolyear, he would always be in the background barking something at her. As soon as he figured out that she was on the phone with me, he always managed to need her for something, causing her to cut our conversation short.

I met a guy during my freshman year at school, who seemed a little too eager for my taste. I knew that he wanted to date me, but I told him that I wasn't interested in anything more than a friendship. He settled for that and we became good friends. Persistence and patience paid off for him; we ended up dating senior year. A year after we graduated, he slowly started to change. He became more possessive and more jealous.

Ava:

After a few failed attempts at dating, I met this dude that appeared to be just what the doctor ordered and exactly what I'd prayed for. The guy that I dated before him was a closet freak; I still don't know if he was bi-sexual or homosexual. What wasn't cool was that he hid it from me. I, unfortunately, had to find out the hard way. The next morning, I asked God where all the normal guys were. Two weeks later, he answered. God literally put a man right on my doorstep; my new mailman. He told me that his name is Brian and that they changed his route.

I knew that he was attracted to me. On weekends, when I was home, I usually kept my screen door locked with my main door open, because my main door had the mail slot, and he'd have no access to shove my mail into the door. This meant that Brian had to ring my bell to give me my mail.

Usually, I timed my workouts to be finished right around the time that Brian would be delivering my mail. You best believe that I made sure that I had my tiniest running shorts on with a cute sports bra. I'd have my hair in a ponytail and have a fresh coat of lip-gloss on. He'd ring the doorbell and I'd rush to the door as if I was preoccupied. I knew he would drool as soon as he saw me. It never failed; I'd go to the door looking sweaty and sexy and he'd try his hardest to strike up a conversation.

Instances like this went on for about a month. When I felt like I had baited him enough, I put my plan into action. The next time that he was scheduled to deliver my mail, I made sure that I wasn't home. I did this for about two weeks straight. I was positive that he would be looking for me. That's exactly what I wanted; I wanted him to be thinking about me, to think about our conversations, and I wanted him to miss me.

On the third week, I timed it so it appeared that I would be leaving in a rush when he delivered my mail. This time I was dressed as if I was going on a date. He knew what I looked like after a workout, but had no idea what I looked like after I cleaned up. I knew that he'd ask me out by this point, because for all he knew, he might not run into me again. He didn't strike me as dumb enough to miss that opportunity.

I'm sure he must have thought I was rushing to meet some other dude. That's what I wanted him to think. As expected, he asked me out to dinner. I lied and told him that he totally caught me off guard, that I had no idea that he was interested in me. I knew he was more than interested. In fact, I'm sure he wanted to devour me. I acted shy and unaware of his attraction to me as I agreed to go out with him the following weekend.

Brian picked me up in a silver compact car. I don't even know what it was. It was something that KIA made. I can't say I was expecting him to have a small car. I asked God for normal and that's what he gave me. We went to the Olive Garden in South Bay. The one thing that turned me off is that he calculated the tip down to the penny. Damn, did he think it would be a sin to give the waiter more than the customary percentage?

After we ate, we went to Revere Beach, where we walked and talked for about an hour, and then he took me home. I let him kiss me good night. This kiss was all right, I guess; it didn't provide any moisture to my panties, but at the same time, it didn't qualify as a bad kiss. Like I said, the kiss was alright.

By date number four, I was tired of the light fondling that we'd graduated to. I had invited him over and intended to turn him out. I'd had a lot of practice by this time. I had become very skillful. I had not had the opportunity to practice on anyone since the closet freak. So I did anything and everything with Brian that night. It had been a few months since I'd had sex and those few months of celibacy had me feeling as if I was practically a virgin. I had a lot of making up to do. To my pleasant surprise, Brian aimed to please and his dick had great aim! I forgot all about that tip incident.

Evelyn:

Now that I was in a committed relationship with a man that was my friend first, I felt secure. I really had high hopes that this relationship would last and turn into the opposite of what my mom had with my dad. I wanted this to be a healthy relationship. We took time to get to know each other before we became a couple.

When I finished getting dressed for work and was on my way out the door, he asked me to change my outfit. John stayed the night at my place. He was acting kind of weird. Actually it wasn't weird. It was jealousy that was clouding his judgment. This idiot was really pushing my buttons; he actually demanded that I change my clothes. He said that my outfit was too tight for work. I looked at him as if he must be playing.

I never had anyone ever tell me that I dressed too provocatively. I ignored his comment and continued to get ready to leave for work. It was only 2 pm and he had a drink in his hand. I noticed that he was drinking more; he wasn't drinking enough to label him an alcoholic, but it was enough that I noticed it. I told him that I didn't want to be late and therefore, I was not going to change my outfit. Next thing you know, my outfit was dripping wet with his brown liquor. He'd lost his mind; he actually took his Hennessy and splashed it on my outfit.

He had the nerve to tell me that if I thought I was going to be late before, I was really going to be late now. I really couldn't believe that he threw his drink at me. I looked at my cream top in disbelief. My breasts were damp, yet the heat from my temper is what I felt the most.

At the top of my lungs, I ordered him to get out of my motherfucking house and to lose my fucking number. He left without saying a word, but made sure he slammed the door so hard that he shook the black and white artwork on my walls.

I didn't speak to John for a week. He sent me flowers and a card with a long handwritten apology. He blamed it on the alcohol and professed his love to me; he said that he couldn't live without me and begged me to forgive him. I wanted to believe that it had to be the alcohol, because I'd never seen him behave that way in all the years that I'd known him. I wanted to believe that nobody in their right mind would behave that way, so I forgave him.

The night that I forgave him, he came over and made love to me with so much passion; he actually cried during our lovemaking. I knew that he was sorry and I saw no reason to punish him or ever bring the Hennessy incident up again. We both just acted as if it never happened.

I didn't see him take another drink in my presence for an entire month after our short breakup. I later learned that just because I didn't see it, didn't mean that he wasn't doing it. A few weeks later, I had a black eye to prove it. What hurt more than the black eye was that when I looked in the mirror, I didn't see myself; I was looking at my mother.

THE BITTER PAST

Ava's relationship before Brian:

We were both continuing our education. I was getting my master's in business and he was getting his bachelors in psychology. We met in the library at the university. We hit it off right from the start. We had many thought-provoking conversations about everything and anything going on under the sun.

Although we were both the same age, we were on a different academic pace. After high school, he waited three years before starting undergrad. Four years later, he's finishing his bachelors on the Dean's list. While he was doing that, I was struggling to maintain a solid B-average in my business courses. We joked about how we were both the same age and graduating at the same time, but I was leaving with a masters.

Once we graduated, we had the whole summer to find real jobs and start the rest of our life. Neither one of us could find jobs in our field, so we both applied for a job at a marketing firm; he got it and I didn't. I ended up working at a local retail store and actively submitted my resume for other job opportunities.

Each day we'd call each other and talk about how our workday went and then schedule a time to meet at the end of the week. While we were still in school, we went to the movies a lot and to inexpensive fast food places to talk about the movie.

Lately, when I suggested going to the movies and out to eat, he claimed he was busy. This was happening way too much for my liking. I told him that he didn't have to lie to me; if he wasn't feeling me anymore, just let me know. He said that he was still feeling me and that I should stop being paranoid.

On a Wednesday night, after he declined another offer to hang out, I called my girlfriends Evelyn and Charlene. Paranoid my ass! Something wasn't right and I always trust my gut instincts. I asked my girls to come and get me so we could see just what this liar of mine was up to.

When he left his apartment that night, I was expecting to see him meet up with another woman, but surprisingly, I didn't. He walked to his car with a black duffel bag, which could easily serve as an overnight bag. When he got into his Honda Accord, we followed him all the way down I-93 South to I-95. Next thing you know, we are in Rhode Island.

Shit was getting interesting. My MAC glossed lips slowly parted. My mouth was wide open. I was more than shocked when I saw where he was going; this dude was going into a gay club. My girls wanted to go in and see what was up. I was in too much shock to move. I stood there with my mouth open, thinking, *how could he be gay and I didn't pick up on it?* If he was gay, he was straddling the fence big time. We did all types of things together in the bedroom and he enjoyed every minute of it; I made sure of that.

My girls went into the club without me. I sat in the car, trying to rack my brain for signs that I might have missed. When they came back, they were cracking up; Charlene was laughing so hard that she had tears in her eyes. They said that I needed to go in.

I told them that I didn't want to see my gay boyfriend hitting on some man, but my girls weren't trying to hear it. They said that they drove me all this way, so I better go in and confront him. At first, I thought about checking these bitches. *Who did they think that they were talking to?* Then, I checked myself; after all, they did drop everything that they were doing to stalk my boyfriend for me.

The place was dimly lit and smelled like cigarettes and weed. *I thought that we couldn't smoke in public buildings anymore.* I looked around and he was nowhere to be found; I figured he probably spotted me and dipped out before I got a chance to see him. Making my way to the door, I heard the deejay introduce the male strippers. The first stripper received such an overwhelming applause that I had to see what he was working with. When I turned around, I found out why I couldn't find my boyfriend.

That closet freak must have been getting ready for his performance when I was looking for him. *This was his job?* Shaking his ass in a G-string for some loot was his job! He never got the marketing job. He'd lied to me so that I wouldn't question where his money was coming from.

I walked up to the stage and stood there staring in horror as some fat, sloppy-looking, white guy put a couple of singles in his G-string. When he finally realized I was standing there, he stopped dancing and just looked at me. The crowd didn't know what was going on, but they weren't feeling me interrupting the show. I said nothing; I gave him the finger and walked out. He never called me again and I never saw him again; I still don't know if he's into men. Three months later, I met Brian.

Charlene's relationship before Derek:

We met on the internet; I told the truth in my profile and he lied in his. We met up at a Dunkin Donuts in Kendall Square. Gratefully, he looked exactly like his picture did on his page. He was basketball player tall, and had a smooth chocolate complexion. His hair was curly like the old school R&B singer Al B. Sure. One thing that stood out is that he didn't talk much; he let me do all the talking. When he did chime in, he was funny. He told me that he was a good catch, so I'd better not mess up. He said he had a great job and if I acted right, he would to take me to dinner the following night.

That was his way of asking me out on a second date. I agreed to go to dinner. I ended up having a great time! Each time we went out, I had a great time. This man took me to plays and museums. We went to upscale restaurants and never had to wait in line at clubs. He was perfect.

After a while, I realized that I knew nothing about him, except for what I'd learned from his page online. We liked the same things. He was funny, courteous, and he always left me wanting for more. The weird thing was that he never talked about his family or about his job.

All he said was that he was a consultant for a pharmaceutical company and didn't have a lot of family. It troubled me when I realized that I hadn't done my research, but I kept dating him and noticed that he never really answered my questions, at least not the important ones.

Turns out, this man was no pharmaceutical consultant. He was a drug dealer! He didn't sell weed. He was selling pills, lots and lots of pills. I found this out the hard way, after having a lovely meal at one of his favorite restaurants. We were driving to Revere Beach and on our way there, we get stopped by the state police. I'll admit, we weren't going the speed limit, but we weren't going that fast. I figured this would just be a routine traffic stop; he'd get a ticket or maybe get lucky and get a warning.

My guestimation was waaaaaay off; I almost ended up in jail that night. This fool had a trunk full of pills and a warrant out for his arrest; so the cop let me go and arrested him. I took a cab home. As soon as I got home, I got down on my knees and thanked God that I wasn't arrested. I called my girlfriends to fill them in and to let them get their laugh on at my expense. After that nightmare, there was no more internet dating for me. Eight months later, I meet Derek at a flea market.

Evelyn's relationship before Fritz:

I thought he was going to kill me. Nobody was around and it was late. He worked in a remote area, so the building was vacant. Nobody, and I mean nobody would hear me if I screamed In fact, when I did scream, nobody heard me. This amused him. I had to think fast. He had me pinned to the floor with his knee on my neck. It was at this point that I painfully realized I was dealing with someone that had more than a few screws loose. It didn't help his screw deficit that he had a few too many to drink also.

34

With tears in my eyes, I apologized for whatever it was that set him off. Then I flipped the script and started begging him not to leave me. It sounds crazy to ask a crazy man not to leave you, but it was necessary if I wanted to live. Although I was scared, I had to be smart. This man had lost his mind and he was hell-bent on not losing me. In the back of my mind, I knew I was going to leave him, but I was certain that he wasn't going to let me go so easily.

I was dealing with a crazy individual who was obsessed with me and I had to make it seem as though I still wanted him. I couldn't let him feel rejected, because that fueled his craziness. I was finally able to convince him that I loved him. When he released me, I silently thanked God because only God could deliver me from something like that. With his permission, I went into the bathroom to do an inspection. I looked ok enough not to warrant any questions from anyone.

Before I met this man, I was not in favor of the death penalty. He quickly changed that. That night when we got home, he acted as if nothing had happened and actually expected me to give him some. I didn't want a repeat of his knee to my neck, so I did. I really didn't want to, but doing that seemed like a better idea than dealing with the consequences of the alternative.

From that point on, I plotted my exit out of his life. I couldn't commit myself to a life with a man that was abusive, with serial killer tendencies. One would have never imagined that this man was my friend before he became my man. By the time I finally had enough courage to end the relationship, I was underweight and stressed the hell out. I never knew that I could get so stressed that I had no appetite for weeks. The twenty-five pounds I'd lost being stressed wasn't a good look.

I honestly thought about killing him in his sleep. Fortunately for him, the rational woman inside of me decided that she didn't want to spend any time in jail over him. Eventually, I was successful with ending the relationship. It wasn't easy, by any means of the imagination; I went through a lot of abuse during the time I was trying to figure out how I was going to escape this relationship.

Reflecting back on some of the terrible things he did to me, made me question my scruples. What was I doing with a man like this? After he splashed the Hennessy on my blouse, I shouldn't have given him another chance. This man was evil, crazy and had done cruel things to me.

The demon poured a blender full of cold water on me after I came home from the hair salon, because he said I was acting as if I was cute. On another occasion, he'd bitten the inside of his cheek while eating a meal I prepared for him. Of course, it was my fault that he bit his cheek. This piece of shit of a man decided to bite me, because I told him that he was acting like a baby. He decided to make it a point to show me his baby side by biting me so hard I thought that I was going to pass out from the pain.

I can't remember the reason why, but he spit in my face on another occasion. This psychotic motherfucker destroyed the art collection I had with a butcher's knife, because he thought I cared more about my paintings than about him. I had no idea I was dealing with Lucifer in the flesh!

He was getting crazier by the day. I will never forget the day we were driving over the Zakim Bridge. He was mad at the way the wind blew that morning and to him, it was obvious that I must have had something to do with it. He grabbed the gear shaft in my car and rammed it from drive into park while I was going sixty miles per hour. He did this a few times down the highway; I had an impossible time driving and trying to keep him from shifting my automatic gears.

He eventually got his kicks out of it and stopped. I am not sure if it was because he got tired of doing it or he realized that if I got stuck out on the highway, so would he. Needless to say, the damn fool destroyed my transmission.

I agreed to go with him to visit his 85-year-old aunt one weekend. While we were there, he got upset about what I chose to wear that day. The knee length pencil-skirt that I had on all day all of a sudden was too short and tight for him. When I rolled my eyes at him, he attacked me at his aunt's house! Lucky for me, the neighbors heard me. Thank God again, for their intervention.

This fool wouldn't give me my pocketbook and I left without it. That wasn't the first time that he'd held my pocketbook hostage. I'd gotten into the habit of keeping my money and credit cards on me. He had my keys, but I had spares hidden.

I left his aunt's house with a fat, bloody lip. I cried as I walked down the street, heading towards the Ashmont train station. *How had my life become such a mess?* Once I made it home, I avoided everyone. He tried calling and apologizing. He sent me flowers, but when I wouldn't give in, he started terrorizing me. He threatened and stalked me. My nerves were shot to hell. It got to the point where Ava had her cousin Craig intervene. I don't know what he said to him, but all of the drama stopped after Craig visited him. Thank God for them; I considered Ava and Craig more than just friends, they were family to me. A year later, I met Fritz.

OUR RELATIONSHIPS

Ava and Brian:

It's supposed to be a quiet, peaceful Tuesday night at the house. Tonight, however; my husband, Brian, is invading my space. I can hear him going back and forth between his study and the living room. He religiously goes out with some of his co-workers from the postal office and bowls on Tuesdays. Tonight, he's home and I don't know why.

I was looking forward to a night free of complaints. Tuesday nights were the nights I looked forward to; I dedicated those nights to me. I was free to do whatever, but I preferred to stay at the crib. I enjoyed having the house to myself.

So far, he hasn't complained. I don't know if it counts, because he has not said a word since he moped through the door. This is fine with me; I honestly didn't want to be bothered. Lately, he's been complaining about his job more than usual. He's been putting me in a sour mood with all his bitching. I can't share anything about my day, because he does enough complaining for the both of us.

Finally, he asks what's for dinner. I tell him that I don't cook on Tuesday nights. We both usually eat out, because he's out with his friends and I'm doing me. I ask him why he's not out bowling and he says, "I'm just not feeling it tonight."

Something's up. He never misses his Tuesday night bowling. I decide to leave it alone and retreat to the bedroom. We may be in the same house, but I don't have to be in the same room with him. I planned on ordering some take out, playing some reggae and reading the new book I purchased over the weekend.

I was praying he would just keep to himself and leave me the hell alone for the night. I tense up when he knocks on the bedroom door and asks if I want something from the Chinese food spot, because he's ordering. I don't get up to answer the door. I yell through the door, "Get me the number seven combination plate." He says, "Okay," and leaves.

Ten minutes later, he comes back to the door and yells, "I'm about to leave, and your portion comes to eight fifty-nine." I couldn't believe this man. He is so cheap! He really waited outside of the door for me to give him my portion of the money owed for my meal. I got up out of the bed, threw my book on the nightstand and pulled a ten-dollar bill out of my purse to give my husband. I opened my locked bedroom door and said, "Bring me back my change."

He walked away and didn't say anything. This man is so cheap; it's sickening. I must have fallen asleep reading the book. When I woke up, my food was on my nightstand. There was also a note that said he'd changed his mind and left to go bowl. I was glad, but unhappy that he didn't leave my change like I'd asked.

Brian got home later than usual. I didn't question it because he got off to a late start last night. I was in a better mood this morning, and I asked him how his night went. He starts telling me that he's glad that he decided to go out because he needed to relieve some stress.

On that note, I started to tune him out. I wasn't in the mood to listen to all the reasons why he was stressed. He's that type of person that you can never top. If you had a bad day, your day couldn't be worse than his was.

It's 7 am, and I am running late for work. Brian has left for work already. I don't know why it takes me so long to get my outfit together. My grandfather told me once that I should put my clothes out for the week on Sunday night. That way, I won't be late for work trying to figure out what to wear. Did I listen? Well, I listened, but didn't apply it.

For some reason, when Sunday night gets here, I never feel like planning out my outfits for the week. It just seems so overwhelming. Who feels like ironing five outfits in one night? I know I don't. I finally got my outfit together and I go in the bathroom mirror to take one last look at myself. While I'm in there, I notice that the toilet paper roll is empty.

Brian knows how much I hate it when he leaves me sitting on the toilet with no toilet paper. So, to avoid an argument, I look underneath the sink for a roll. I'm shocked when I pull the roll of toilet paper out, because behind the toilet paper is a box of feminine wipes. I'm shocked, because I didn't buy these wipes. I sit down on the toilet seat stumped. I can't figure out why there are feminine wipes that I didn't buy under my sink.

I call my husband on his cell phone. When he answers, he sounds like he's walking because I can hear the wind blowing. I assume he's already on his mail route.

"Brian, there are feminine wipes under the sink."

"And . . ."

"And I didn't put them there," I said with an attitude.

"That's because I did."

"Why would you put feminine wipes under the sink, Brian?"

"The last time you sent me to the store to pick up some pads, I bought them too."

"Brian, that was three weeks ago when I sent you. I've been under this sink a million times since then. These wipes haven't been here for three weeks!"

"I know," he says. "They must have fallen out in my trunk when I took the bag with your pads into the house. A couple of days ago, I noticed they were in my trunk. So, I brought them in and put them under the sink for you."

"I don't use those. Why would you buy them when I didn't ask for them?"

"I don't know. It seemed right at the time and they were on sale. I know how much you like a good sale. So, I bought them. Damn! Why are you bothering me on my route with this stuff? I try to do a thoughtful thing and you're giving me the third degree!"

"Well, I'm sorry, Brian. Let's be real. You have never seen me buy any feminine wipes, nor did I ask you to. You picked a weird way to show that you can be thoughtful."

"Ava, you really don't give me enough credit," Brian said and then disconnected the call.

I thought about calling him back to cuss him out for hanging up on me, but I was officially late for work trying to figure this out. In a weird kind of way it was thoughtful of him, but I wondered if I should I be insulted. Was he trying to tell me something by buying me feminine wipes?

When I get to work, I emailed the girls to tell them to call me so that I can tell them what happened this morning. Evelyn is the first one to call me back. While I'm telling her the story,

Charlene beeps in. I don't answer; I wait until she hangs up and then tell Evelyn that I'm going to conference Charlene in. She obviously looked at her caller ID, because she greets me with, "Bitch, you saw it was me calling."

Evelyn and I couldn't help but laugh. When I finished telling them the story, Charlene says to me, "Girl, your coochie smell that bad that your man is buying you wipes?"

I really can't stand Charlene sometimes. I changed the subject and asked "So, where's your fiancé working at these days, Charlene?"

"He's still at the same place."

"Wow, that's good for him. He's almost been there three months" Evelyn says.

"I really don't know what his problem is. I threatened him. I've even told him that I wouldn't marry him if he kept quitting jobs like he does," Charlene says with frustration in her voice. "I mean seriously, why can't he stay put?"

Neither one of us says anything. We both know that Charlene loves Derek, but she's been going back in forth with her decision to marry him. She said that she didn't grow up poor and didn't want to live her adult life poor.

My man is cheap, but he pays his portion of the bills. That's one thing I never had to deal with before and don't want to start now. If he switched jobs like Derek, I'd be a nervous wreck. It's a good thing Charlene doesn't need his money, but it would be nice if she could count on it if she needed it though.

I personally, think that she is settling. And she is the last person that needs to settle. She's beautiful, educated, and can take care of herself. Evelyn says she has to get back to work, so we all agree to hang up and hang out with each other before the month is over.

Charlene and Derek:

"Ain't nothing going on but the rent! You gotta have a J-O-B if you wanna be with me. No romance without finance," Gwen Guthrie's voice sang aloud as I sat in my car listening to my satellite radio. I laughed and thought about making that song my ringtone. My wedding is three months away and I still haven't lost the weight that I wanted to. I told myself that I would lose ten more pounds. This was definitely doable within the next three months.

I still haven't found a dress, either. Ava thinks I'm crazy and that I should have picked out a dress by now. None of them seem to fit me right or feel right. Maybe it's a sign that I shouldn't be getting married. Who knows?

I called Ava and Evelyn before I left work today and asked them to meet me at a local bridal shop. I'm going to find a dress today, even if I have to try on every dress in the store. I'm already at the bridal shop and both of those heifers are late.

Ava's the first to arrive, rushing in with her designer sunglasses, leather knee-high boots, tight jeans, and a fly, butter-soft leather jacket. She swears she's in a video whenever she's outside of work. Most people come home from work and take off their work clothes to put on more comfortable clothes. Ava comes home from work and puts on her fly clothes.

It's as if she's two different people. Ava's very attractive. She's about 5 feet 7, light skin, long light brown hair, light brown eyes and has an athletic build, but not in a boyish way. Ava has the type of body that spandex looks great on. There are no bumps, lumps or dimples.

Like I said, Ava is fly, but you'd never know she had a fly side if you saw how she dressed for work. Nothing that she wore stood out or was worth complimenting. She wore dark slacks and cotton button-up shirts everyday like it was a uniform. Every once in a while, she would wear a turtleneck.

If you met Ava after 5 pm, it's as if her twin sister came out. Everything that she put on was compliment-worthy. She's the woman that you admire from afar and want to know where she got her shoes, her bag, or her entire outfit.

Anyway, Ava arrived first. She told me that she was going to start gathering her own pile of gowns for me to try on. I told her to go ahead. As Ava was picking out gowns for me, Evelyn strolled in looking snobby as hell.

Don't get me wrong, Evelyn is fly too, but in a quieter way. Evelyn had her clothes tailored to fit her. She wore diamonds and pearls as if they were casual accessories. Evelyn is very classy. She's just about the same height as Ava.

Evelyn is very curvy. She wears her blue-black hair in a slicked back ponytail every day. Her caramel skin always looks sun kissed. I'm sure the routine visits to the spa contribute to that. She doesn't wear a lot of make-up. She wears a nude, glossy lip stain and mascara. That's it and that's all she needs. As snobby as she looks, she is the most down-to-earth person I know. They say never judge a book by its cover. She likes nice things, but is actually very frugal.

Evelyn comes over and gives me a hug. She apologizes for running late and asks how she could assist me. I tell her to start her own pile of gown choices for me like Ava is, and I'll do the same. In fifteen minutes, I'll try them on and they can vote on which gown I should buy. I'm determined to walk out of here with a wedding gown tonight.

Three hours later, we walk out of there with my wedding gown. I convince Ava to let me store it at her house so that Derek doesn't see it. When we leave the dress shop, we are starving and nobody feels like waiting a long time to eat. Going to a sit-down restaurant is not an option tonight, so we opt for pizza.

While we are at the pizza shop, the owner comes out and gives us special attention. I'm not sure, but I think he was feeling Ava, who paid him no mind. After a while, he got the hint and backed off. I was hoping she'd pay him enough attention to get our meal for free. Instead, Ava paid for our meal and we all went our separate ways.

When I got into the car and turned on the satellite radio, TLC's "No Scrubs" was playing. I laughed to myself. *Was God trying to tell me something?* As soon as the song went off, my cell phone beeped, signaling a text message. The text was from Derek.

He said he was running low on cash and needed to go into our rainy day account for fifty bucks. I told him to go ahead. We had more than enough money in there for me not to sweat fifty bucks. We both have been putting money in it every two weeks for some time now.

Evelyn and Fritz:

When I got home, I noticed that Fritz had been by. There were roses for me on the dining room table and a note that said he cooked me dinner. It said he knew that I'd be tired from having such a long day. I opened up the refrigerator to find a plate of rice with vegetables and orange chicken, my favorite. This man is so thoughtful.

I wonder what it is that he wants. Nobody is that nice without wanting something in return. We've been dating for almost a year and a half and he still hasn't slipped up yet. I know he will if I give him time; they all do. I was still full from eating pizza with the girls. I am definitely going to take this meal with me to work tomorrow for lunch.

My birthday is coming up in a week and I have nothing planned. It's not a significant number ending in a zero or a five. I'm going to be twenty-nine next weekend. The girls mentioned clubbing or having a girl's night in. We never decided on anything though; even Fritz hasn't mentioned anything and that's unlike him.

For my last birthday, we flew to the Bahamas for the weekend and lived it up. It was my best birthday ever. Fritz has been busy this past week and hasn't spent as much time at my place as usual. It's not a problem. It's just out of character for him. He's here at least three times a week. He has only been here once this week and that was yesterday when I was out with Ava and Charlene.

As I'm getting ready for work, I call Fritz and tell him that I miss him. He says that he'll take the day off from work if I do and we can spend the day together. I told him as tempting as that sounds, I had to get to work. I had too much going on at the office to take any days off any time soon. I asked him if he was coming over tonight. He said that he would be late, but he'd come by to tuck me in. I couldn't wait; Fritz was very good at tucking me in.

Rushing to get to work, I forgot my orange chicken plate. I realize it when I am halfway to work. There's no way that I am turning around just to get that meal; I'll just have to eat it for dinner tonight. When I get to my desk, I turn on my computer and look in my Outlook calendar. My whole day is full. It's a good thing I didn't bring my lunch; I wouldn't have been able to eat it anyway. Today, I have meetings back-to-back, and luckily, one of them has lunch included.

Finally, my workday is almost over and I only have one meeting left. I've been holding my pee for the last hour; I stop torturing my bladder and head to the bathroom. The closer I get to the bathroom, the more I have to go. It's like my bladder knows that I am almost near a bathroom.

I go into the first stall and start peeing. As I am going pee, someone goes into the stall next to me and starts peeing. First she poots and then she pees. I can't really complain, because we are in the bathroom. If there's any place that it should be okay to poot, it's the bathroom.

Out of nowhere, I smell this strong disgusting smell. Now, I know I washed my coochie this morning before work. It smells like the woman beside me skipped that step in her hygiene routine today. I come out of the stall with my faced scrunched up from the awful odor. I quickly wash my hands, dry them and exit, all while holding my breath.

Once my last meeting is over, I text Ava and Charlene. I tell them that there was this nasty chick in the bathroom today. I told them that her coochie odor was so strong that it stunk up the bathroom and made me run out gasping for air. They both texted me back saying "LMAO". Charlene texted me back again and said "Y'all got some dirty bitches at your job." I texted her back and said, "You are right. We sure do!"

On my way to my car, I ran into my co-worker Becky. Becky told me that she saw what I ate for lunch and that I am brave. I didn't get where she was coming from. So I asked her why she said that I was brave. She said that if she ate that many asparagus her pee would smell like somebody died. I laughed with her, but I was really laughing at myself. I was the one in the bathroom earlier stinking it up.

I'd never eaten asparagus before today. I ended up really liking the taste. Needless to say I overindulged. Nobody ever told me that your urine could smell really bad after eating too many asparagus. Fritz may not be tucking me in tonight. I guess the dirty bitch was me!

Ava:

I'm going over bills and I realize that Brian has not paid the electric bill. I usually don't look at the household bills that he pays, because he's good with his finances. Cheap people usually are good with managing money. This has to be a mistake, because the electric bill says that the last three-month's balances have not been paid. This month, we are responsible for all of it. I wonder what's up that he didn't pay the electric bill for the last three months.

My first instinct is to call or text him, but I decide to wait until he gets home.
It's 11 pm and Brian still has not made it back. By this time, I'm heated. He hasn't called or texted me and I'm too tired to wait up, so I decide to go to sleep.

Its morning time and Brian's lying beside me. I want to smack the shit out of him for being so inconsiderate and not calling last night. I want to ask him where he was and what time he got in, but I don't. I just get up and get ready for work.

Brian's lying in the bed as if he doesn't have to go to work. He is definitely going to be late, because it's 6:30 am and he's still sleeping. Since he didn't feel the need to be considerate last night, I'm not feeling the need to be considerate this morning. *Let his behind oversleep and be late for work.* I continue getting ready for work and then leave without waking him.

All day I wait for a phone call from Brian. I figure he'll at least call to cuss me out for leaving without waking him. Nothing, no calls, no texts; I see he's playing games with me. But, I've got some games up my sleeve too. He better be careful, before I start playing them.

I get home and I see dishes in the sink sitting there like they are going to wash themselves. There are crumbs on the counters and the kitchen table. All of the lights are on in the house, but nobody is in any of the illuminated rooms. The TV is on in our bedroom and there are more food particles on my bedspread and on the nightstand.

I guess Mr. "Don't-Know-How-To-Come-Home or Call" decided to call in sick. A half hour later, Brian graces me with his presence. The look on my face clearly says, "Where the fuck have you been?" Before I could go off on him, my phone rings; it's my Nana. By the time I'm off the phone with Nana, Brian is showered and dressed to go out. It's not Tuesday and even if it were, he wouldn't be wearing a suit. I ask him where he's going and he says that he's going out to meet up with his brother to celebrate his promotion.

I tell him that I didn't know his brother was up for a promotion. Instead of going off, I let things ride and tell him to congratulate his fine ass brother for me. Sometimes I wish I had met his brother instead of him; he's the kind of man I was better suited for. I feel like I got the consolation prize with Brian. Just as that thought entered my head, my lights went out.

I'm way beyond pissed; I have no electricity, so I called Evelyn. Fifteen minutes later, she's outside beeping for me. I'm not staying in this house by myself, with no electricity. *That bastard!*

I was going to leave a note for Brian, but then decided against it. I can't believe he didn't pay the electric bill. Had I not paid my portion of the bills, he would have had a fit. He has a lot of explaining to do. When I get outside, I noticed   Evelyn's car, but she's not in it. It's Fritz who

is driving. Evelyn's lazy behind sent him to get me. It was embarrassing enough to tell her that I

needed to spend the night because my power was out. I didn't want to have to explain my

situation to her man.

"Hi Ava, Evelyn told me that you two planned on having a girls' night in. I hope you

don't mind that I have to make a stop at the liquor store before we get to the house. Evelyn

asked that I bring home some Bacardi so that she could make some drinks."

"No, that's fine, Fritz. I could use a drink."

"Is everything okay Ava?"

"Things are fine, Fritz. Thanks for asking though."

I closed my eyes and listen to the new Brian McKnight CD Fritz is playing. By the time we arrive

at the liquor store, I am half-asleep. Fritz says he'll be right back and I drowsily say, "Okay."

Across the street from the liquor store, I swear I see Brian's brother walk into a fast food place.

I'm half-asleep, so I paid the look-alike no mind and dozed back off to sleep. Brian's

brother was supposed to be out with Brian, celebrating. *That couldn't have been him.* When I

wake up again, we are in front of Evelyn's house. I don't even remember Fritz getting back into

the car from the liquor store.

He opens my door for me and takes my overnight bag. I almost forgot what it was like

for a man to exhibit some chivalry. Brian stopped being a gentleman right after we got married;

in fact, a lot of stuff stopped right after we got married.

Brian used to be so sweet. He was thoughtful and such a joy to be around. We did fun

things together on a regular basis. He bought me gifts, just because. None of that happens

anymore. We hardly do things together and when we do, they aren't fun. He barely remembers

to buy me something on my birthday, never mind buying me something on a whim.

48

As for being a joy to be around, please! I don't know if it's his job or what his problem is, but he's been anything but a joy to be around. The more I think about it, the more pissed I become. All of the things that made me attracted to him no longer existed. It didn't happen overnight; it was a gradual change for the worse. And I gradually started falling out of love with him.

Things haven't been good for a while. I don't know why we are torturing each other. We both make decent money, so we don't need each other for financial reasons. We aren't happy; it's written boldly all over our faces, each time we converse with each other. I never imagined my marriage would become so unfulfilling. Brian and I are definitely overdue for a heart-to-heart talk.

Evelyn:

I could not believe it when Ava called me and said that her lights were out. That was unlike Brian not to pay his bills; Brian has been acting weird lately. He's been doing things out of character. I hope he doesn't have a drug habit that we don't know about.

Fritz was supposed to spend the night, but I cancelled on him when Ava called. He said he understood, but he seemed bummed. He'll get over it; my girl comes first tonight. Ava was full of compliments after Fritz left; she was telling me about how he opened her car door and got her bags. I was listening to her, but in my head I was like, "*What is the big deal?*" He's supposed to do that stuff. Damn, how was she letting Brian treat her?

That's why I am so anti-marriage. All that shit changes once they put a ring on your finger. Fritz has proposed to me two times already and I turned him down. It's not that I don't love him; I just know how things change. I don't want things to change between us. We have a good relationship. I don't need a marriage screwing things up.

"Girl if I was you, I'd marry him tomorrow," Ava says while sipping on her rum and Coke.

"I'm not trying to marry that man, Ava. If I were going to, I would have been engaged by now."

"I don't know what you are scared of."

"I'm scared of having a marriage like yours."

"Okay bitch, now you know that's not fair. Fritz is not Brian. Give him more credit."

"I know he's not Brian, but he could become him. I don't want that."

"Evelyn, you are still letting your ex-fiancé dictate your life and you ain't even with him anymore."

"Ava, you know what I went through with him. I thought I knew him and look how he changed."

"He didn't change, Evelyn. He was like that before; you just missed the signs."

"Well, I would hate to miss the signs again, marry Fritz, and he turn out to be a demon like my ex."

"Every man is not like your ex, Evelyn. Give him the benefit of the doubt. He has not given you any reason to doubt him. If you keep rejecting him, you are going to lose him."

"Oh please; Fritz is not going anywhere," I declare to Ava.

"Okay, enough about men. Tell me more about what eating too much asparagus can do to your pee."

Charlene:

Derek walked in looking and smelling good as usual. It's like he never has a bad day. Everything about him was sexy. His stride was confident. His style of dress was more European than American. He just looked important.

I met Derek at a flea market. I was there looking for unique jewelry and he was there buying a used tire. He saw me looking at a particular piece of jewelry and introduced himself by purchasing it for me. The bracelet was only ten dollars, but that was enough to get my attention. I thought it was sweet. From that day on, we started dating; fast forward to now, and here I am about to be married to him.

Don't get me wrong; Derek does have some flaws. One of the more aggravating flaws is that he quits jobs like they are contagious. Right now he's the manager at a jewelry store. I told him that if he quit this job, I wouldn't marry him. He laughed me off, but I was as serious as a heart attack.

He doesn't have a 401K. He has no savings, IRA's, nothing. This is why we opened a joint account together. He needed to get into the habit of saving money and planning for his future. Speaking of our joint account, I need to go online and check the balance. I key in the website on my laptop and the site says that it is updating the site to make my experience more enjoyable. *I couldn't care less about the site being enjoyable. I just want to check my balance.* Oh well, I will have to wait until tomorrow.

Derek strolls into the living room just as I am shutting the computer down.

"Hey baby," he says and greets me with a kiss.

"Hi hon," I say.

"I was thinking, why don't we go out tonight?" he says while massaging my shoulders.

"Where did you want to go?" I ask.

"We can go to that spot where they do poetry readings."

"No thanks, I think I'll pass on that invite tonight."

"Okay well, let's stay in then. I can cook you something to eat and then give you a bath."

"Now that sounds more like it. And what will we do after the bath?" I say seductively.

"We can read some poetry together," he says jokingly.

He and I laugh, both knowing what's going down after or during the bath.

Ava:

The next day, I arrived at home to find the electricity back on. All night I had talked shit to Evelyn about how I was going to go off on him for having me up in the house with no electricity, while he was out all night celebrating.

Again, when I got home, there was no one to go off on. He must have gone to work early. I don't blame him for not wanting to hear what I was about to say to him. I was so worked up last night, I even dreamed about going off on him. It's Saturday, so if he took a shift today, he should be back early.

I think I'll stay put until he comes home. I call my hairdresser and tell him that I am not feeling well so I need to cancel my standing appointment. I then call the girls and tell them that I won't be meeting them for our late lunch today. Brian was not going to be able to avoid me. We are going to talk today. He should be home by one o'clock. I fall asleep, waiting on Brian, When I wake up, it's three pm. I can't believe I slept that long.

Where is he? An hour later, he is still not home. I get tired of waiting and decide to go to the mall. When I get there, I go straight to Macy's and head to the MAC counter. I was running low on my eye shadow and lipstick. After I bought my cosmetics; I headed to the shoe section. I was feeling down and there's nothing like a pair of new shoes to pick you right up. I left Macy's with two new pairs of heels and a new pocketbook.

As I was heading out, I thought I saw Brian's brother. I followed him so that I could get a closer look to see if it was him. It was him alright.

"Hey Ben!" He turns around to see who is calling his name. When he notices it is me, he smiles.

"Hi Ava. How have you been?"

"I've been okay. I hear you are doing well."

He looks at me funny and says, "What's that supposed to mean?"

I say, "Brian told me about your new promotion."

He looks at me funny again and says, "Ava, you are about 8 months late. I almost forgot I got promoted."

I laugh on the outside, but cringe on the inside.

"Well, I figure better late than never."

"I guess you are right. Thanks for your belated congratulations."

"Well, I was just saying hello. I gotta get going. It was good seeing you. I'll be sure to tell Brian I saw you." *You better believe I'm going to tell him I saw Ben.*

"You be sure to do that. I've been trying to get Brian to spend some time with his big brother for months now. You seem to be taking up a lot of his free time in the evenings. I can't say I blame him for wanting to spend his free time with his beautiful wife."

I feel my cheeks getting warm as if I'm blushing. He thinks I'm blushing from the compliment, but I am really blushing out of anger from the fact that my husband has been lying. He's lied to his brother about spending time with me and he's lied to me about spending time with him.

53

I give Ben a hug and a kiss and immediately pick up my cell phone to call Charlene and Evelyn on my way to my car. Neither of them answers their phone. I decide that it is probably for the best. I need to do some investigating before I let them know what's going on anyway.

It's a frigid Monday morning and I call in sick. I get dressed as if I'm going to work. I put on my slacks and my white pinstriped button-up shirt. I walk out of the house at the regular time I leave every Monday through Friday. My plan is to head over to Budget and rent a car for a few days. On my way to Budget, I drive in the direction of the post office, hoping to see my husband's car at work. Instead, I see one of his co-workers.

She notices me casing the post office employee parking lot. She comes up to my window and greets me. Her high pitched voice is always irritating as hell. It's extra irritating so early in the morning. She starts talking about how good it is to see me and how she's sorry about Brian. She said that they miss him at work, but really miss him on Bowling Night.

My head was spinning. *What was she talking about? He was just at the bowling alley last week with them. Wasn't he? Isn't that what he told me?* The more she spoke, the more stupid I felt. When she was done, I told her it was good seeing her and that I was sure Brian missed them too.

I finally make my way to Budget and have tears in my eyes. My gut tells me that I know that I am not going to like what I am looking for, but I am compelled to find out for myself what is going on with my lying-ass husband. I get in my economy car and head back to the house. I decide to go with my gut today. My gut told me to park a couple of houses down from my house and I will see Brian coming back to the house after he thinks I am at work.

I know that if it was me and I was up to something, I would call my wife's job number to find out if she was actually there. If he did, he would know that I called out sick. I'm not worried however, because I know he won't call. Just as I suspected, he showed back up at the house at 10 am with a Dunkin Donut coffee cup in his hand.

I wait outside and see what he is going to do next. A half hour later, he comes outside dressed in a sweat suit and sneakers as if he's going to the gym. He gets in his car and drives off. I follow along behind him. The last time that I followed a man was when we ended up at the gay strip club. I wonder where I will end up this morning.

We end up in Dorchester. Where the hell was he going? He pulls up to an apartment complex right on Blue Hill Avenue. It looks like Section 8 housing. I drive past him and park in a spot further up the street, but not so far that I can't see him if he gets out through my rear view mirror. Two minutes later, a petite Hispanic looking chick comes out of the apartment complex and gets into my husband's car. I can't see anything at this point. Soon they drive off and so do I.

Now I am two cars behind them. They get back on the highway and head back north. When they finally stop, they are in front of the gym. He actually drove to Dorchester to pick this chick up to go to the gym. He better have a side hustle as a trainer; that's all I'm saying.

I sit in my car steaming! I'm in the gym's parking lot stalking my husband. An hour later, they both get back into my husband's car and end up back at our house. I park a few houses down and watch as my husband and this chick walk into our home.

I give them ten minutes and then I head in. I don't hear anything at first when I walk in. I make sure to be extra quiet, because I don't want to give the bitch a head start from getting away from me. My gut is flipping; I know something is about to go down. I look around and I see no signs of them. I head up to my bedroom and don't see them, but my bathroom door is closed and I hear the shower going.

The bathroom is foggy; good thing I didn't get my hair done, because the steam would have torn my head up. I only see one shadow in the shower and not a lot of movement. I say to myself, *where did she go? Did she leave before and I just missed her?* I open the shower door and quickly find out why I only saw one shadow.

55

My husband had his back towards me when I opened the shower door. His butt cheeks were clenched and the petite woman was on her knees giving some serious head to my husband. Neither one of them noticed me standing there.

I turned the water all the way on hot and got their undivided attention. They both screamed as the hot shower water burned their asses. When they noticed me standing there, they both screamed again. Neither one of them knew what to do. I left them in the shower and walked out of the bathroom with both of their clothes and all the towels.

When they came out they had to come out naked. I took pictures of both of them. I was going to divorce this bastard and I wanted proof of his adultery; I preferred taking pictures rather than my proof coming from a clinic informing me that I had a sexually transmitted disease.

Evelyn:

Today is my birthday. The girls are supposed to be taking me out on the town later tonight. Fritz told me that he was taking me out to dinner. When I asked where, he wouldn't tell me. He said it was a surprise. I wasn't really excited; another year has passed and my life really hasn't changed much. I guess I should be grateful, but somehow I felt like everyone else was enjoying life and here I was just living.

We get to the restaurant and it is packed; I asked him if we had reservations. He said we did, but I couldn't understand why they had us waiting ten minutes if we had reservations. As we stood in the foyer of the restaurant, I bitched and moaned about everything. I was in such a foul mood; too foul for it to be my birthday. I just couldn't help it, I really didn't feel like celebrating.

Five minutes later, we are heading to our seats. I'm in such a funk, I don't even realize that I am passing my family and friends. They were all seated at individual tables like a reception. When I see Ava and Charlene, I know something's up, but before I could get a word out, the entire restaurant yells, "Surprise!" I am beyond shocked. I turn to Fritz and tell him, "Thank you." My mood softened and I enjoyed my birthday party.

Right before dinner was served; Fritz gets up and says that he wants to say a few words to my family and friends; I tell him to go ahead. What I didn't know was that I was giving him permission to embarrass himself. Long story short, Fritz proposed to me in front of everyone. I said, "No," and the whole mood changed.

People were shocked. The entire room got quiet with a sad and awkward silence. Fritz thought I was joking, but I was serious. *He knew that I wasn't ready for marriage. Why did he ruin my birthday with this marriage crap? Things are going great between us. Why is he trying to mess up a good thing with marriage?*

Fritz leaves my side and walks towards the door without turning back to look at me. Before he leaves, he walks over to my girls and says something while giving them a hug. That was three weeks ago. I haven't seen him since.

When he walked out of my birthday party, he walked out of my life. I really couldn't believe that he could abandon me like that. He hasn't called me and he hasn't answered my calls. He just quit me cold turkey. This was something that I definitely wasn't use to. I never said that I didn't love Fritz; I just couldn't marry him. Why couldn't he just accept that?

He is so selfish. His way or no way; how could he just throw us away? It's been a month and still no Fritz. At first, I was sad and hurt, but now I'm just plain pissed. How could he act like I never existed? Doesn't he even miss me? How could you want to marry someone one day and then the next you forget you ever knew them?

There were no phone calls, no emails, no letters, no unannounced visits, nothing. I stopped trying to reach him after the first week. I mean, I loved him, but I wasn't desperate. I definitely don't want any man that doesn't want me.

Charlene:

The wedding is six weeks away. Everything is in order. We just have to make a couple of payments in the next few weeks. Derek and I are paying for the majority of the wedding ourselves. I'll be done paying my portion of the wedding costs we agreed to split by next week. I'm not sure how much more Derek has to pay, but he's assured me that things are in order and all that I need to focus on is showing up and looking pretty.

Derek felt that I was movie star gorgeous. He said that when he first saw me he thought I could have been Zoe Saldana's twin sister. We have the same body type, same almond eyes and the same black hair color and texture. The only difference was that I was darker. I am the same color as Rudy from *The Cosby Show.*

It's hard for me not to have my hand in all the details of the wedding; I just don't want anything to mess up. It's a special day and I don't want any bad surprises. When I give other people too much control, they usually disappoint me and I really don't want to be disappointed on my wedding day. I know everything is going to work out; I am just stressing for no reason.

I know Derek is no Brian, but Ava really had me thinking twice about marrying Derek. She didn't know that she was planting doubt in my mind, but the more she told me about what happened between Brian and her, the more I began to get nervous about Derek. Brian is good looking, but Derek is gorgeous.

What would I do if some tramp tried to steal my husband behind my back? What would I do if I caught Derek with another woman? I have no idea how I would react. Marriage is different from dating. When a boyfriend cheats, you kick him to the curb. When your husband cheats, kicking him to the curb becomes complicated. There are always other things to consider.

Again, here I go stressing. I am thinking about things that I don't need to be thinking about. Derek and I will be married the end of next month, and we will have a good marriage; we will not be like Ava and Brian. We will be Mr. and Mrs. Derek Hilton.

I can't wait for the honeymoon. I think I am looking more forward to that than the actual wedding. We are going to Jamaica for eight days; I've never been there, but I hear it is beautiful. When we get back, we will start house hunting.

I need to go online and check on the accounts, especially our joint rainy day account. As I am logging on, Derek strolls in.

"Hey babe, Whatcha doing?"

"Nothing, I was just about to log on to our accounts. I haven't been on our joint account's website in a while."

"Oh, okay, well when you're done, you wanna go for a walk on the beach?"

"It's kind of chilly out tonight, Derek."

"Okay, well how about we go to Chili's for appetizers?"

"Now that sounds good. We can go now. I'll log on later tonight or tomorrow."

"Okay, I'll be in the car waiting."

Derek and I drive to Chili's and we jammed to the new Mary album all the way there. Ironically, Derek is a Mary J. Blige fan like me. He has all of her albums. I've never met a man that loved Mary as much as I do. He earned major cool points when I discovered he was a

Mary fan.

Derek likes a lot of the same things that I like, one of the reasons we get along so well. The only time we clash is when it comes to his employment or lack of. For some reason, Derek can't stay employed at the same place for more than three or four months. I don't know if it is something psychological, or if he just gets tired of working and quits.

He's been at the jewelry store for almost six months now. That's the longest period of time that he's been employed with the same company since I've met him. He still has a college kid mentality, except he didn't finish college.

He still wants to hang out Thursday through Sunday. Having a career doesn't seem to fit into his life. I don't get it; when he asked me to marry him, I told him that as much as I love him, I couldn't see myself marrying someone that I had to worry about all the time regarding his employment. That would stress me the hell out. My fiancé promised that he would keep the next job that he got and I promised to marry him if he did.

When he started working, he gave me half of his check to put towards the wedding. He did that for six straight weeks. After that, I came up with the idea of opening up a rainy day joint account. That was my way of telling him that I wanted to build a life with him and that I trusted him.

That was short lived. Derek stopped giving me half of his check. He promised that he'd save his money in his own savings account. He told me that he was grown and didn't need to hand over his check like an irresponsible teenager. I agreed with him.

We should have a good chunk of money in there by now. I'm really proud of him. This is a big change for him. Before we met, he didn't have a bank account, didn't save his money, and he cashed his check at local check cashing store.

His rent is split three ways, because he lives with two other roommates. The only bill he ever worried about paying was his rent. Everything else got paid if he had it. That's how he managed his life; he would say, "If I ain't got it, they can't get it."

I don't know how many times I've told him not to make bills that he knew he couldn't afford to pay. That way of thinking was very scary to me; and we have had several long talks since then about managing our finances. I'm happy for him; I think he's finally on his way to becoming a financially responsible citizen.

Ava:

"I'm divorcing Brian."

"Ha, ha, ha, stop playing, Ava. What did he do now?" Evelyn asks.

"He had some young chick from Dorchester all up in my house, in my shower, performing oral sex on him. From the sounds my husband was making, she was doing a damn good job."

"What!" Evelyn hollers in disbelief.

"Yup my husband has a girlfriend. Can you believe it?"

"No, I can't. Did you really catch them in the act?"

"Butt clenched on his way to an orgasm in the act," I say bitterly.

"I just can't believe this. I mean I knew you two had your differences, but not like this."

"Yeah, this caught me off guard too, but now things are starting to make sense."

"What do you mean things are starting to make sense?"

"This fool was lying about everything. Remember the night I spent over at your house when our lights got cut off? Well, that night he was supposed to be out with his brother, celebrating a promotion. This fool lied. I ran into his brother Ben at the mall and he told me that he got a promotion over eight months ago. He went on to say that he's been trying to get Brian to spend some time with him, but that devil claimed that he was spending his time with me."

"I'm sure there is some rational explanation, Ava."

"Yeah, the explanation is that he was out cheating and he was lying to everyone in the process. Not only that, but he also was laid off. That one took me for a loop, because this fool was getting up and acting like he was going to work every day. I guess he's been living off of his unemployment checks. Having a reduced income and a new young girlfriend must be why our lights were cut off."

"I can't believe you are going through this. Here I am being pissed at a man for wanting to marry me and you are married to a man that obviously doesn't want to be married."

"Evelyn, you know Fritz truly loved you. He's nothing like your crazy ex. Why wouldn't you marry him?"

"Ava, the truth is that I really wanted to marry Fritz."

"So why did you turn him down in front of all your friends and family?"

"I was afraid. I was afraid that he would turn out to be too good to be true. I was scared to take a chance. It's not that he wasn't worth it. I think he would be a great husband, but I was just too shell-shocked to find out what the 'for worse' part could turn into during our marriage."

"You need to get that man back. He's worth fighting for, Evelyn."

"You think that I haven't tried? He won't answer my calls or emails or anything."

"Well it's not like you don't know where he lives. Stop by his house. If he opens his door and allows you to express yourself, then you've still got a chance. If he won't open the door and you know he's home, that means he got someone new and most likely, she's there with him. Either that, or he's over you and doesn't love you anymore. I really don't think he's over you though. I think he's hurt."

"You really think so?

"Listen Evelyn, you decide for yourself if you think he's worth losing because of your fears. Fritz is a good man and you know it. Do you really want someone else to have him?"

"Well . . . no, of course not."

"Good, because I was gonna say that if you didn't want him, I was gonna look him up after I divorce Brian," I said jokingly.

"I bet you would hoe," Evelyn says, cracking up.

After I hung up the phone with Evelyn, I called my grandmother to tell her what was going on and that I planned on divorcing Brian. I didn't give her all of the nasty details, but I told her enough for her to get the picture. I never thought I'd be getting divorced. Then again, I never thought that Brian would ever cheat. I guess anything is possible.

Evelyn:

It's Monday morning; damn, I am late for work already. I didn't sleep well at all; I tossed and turned all night. I kept having nightmares. When I woke up, I expected Fritz to be sleeping beside me, but he wasn't. Although it has been years since I was in an abusive relationship, the nightmares are still fresh.

People mistakenly think that once a woman gets out of an abusive relationship that everything goes back to normal once the abusive man is out of the picture. The physical abuse stops, but the psychological battle scars remain. Nothing ever goes back to normal. The way you live your life changes; you develop paranoia.

It was a month after my ex and I broke up for good. My friends took me out for my birthday. We went to Night Games in Somerville. That night Kid Capri was the guest DJ. The house was packed; any and everybody was there.

Once I got there, I wanted to turn right around and go home. I started to have an anxiety attack. I asked myself what I would I do if my ex showed up. The entire night I watched the door like my life depended on it. From my point of view, my life did depend on it. My girls were irritated by it. They thought I was tripping and couldn't understand why I would spend my birthday night thinking about my ex. I told them that I wasn't purposely thinking about my ex; he haunted me.

Two months later, I went out with my girls to a concert. We had great seats up front. We were seeing my favorite singer Jill Scott. We got there early and were the only ones in our row so far. Slowly folks started filling in. I thought I was seeing things when my ex's cousin had a ticket for a seat in the same row as us. The entire night, all I could think of is that his cousin is going to call my ex and tell him I am here. I spent so much time worrying about that, I couldn't even enjoy Jill's performance. I was afraid of what might be waiting for me after the concert let out.

Luckily, he never showed. After Jill's concert, I wouldn't agree to go out to places that he could possibly show up. I stayed in for months. My girlfriends couldn't understand my reluctance to hang out. If they'd gone through the torture I went through, they'd understand better.

I'm glad they couldn't relate, because I wouldn't wish that experience on anyone. The more I prayed, the stronger and braver I became. Over time, I started hanging out with my girlfriends again, but things never got back to normal for me. Years later and I am having nightmares about this asshole.

I wake up stressed and with a headache each time I dream about him. I have no idea where he is or what he's doing with himself these days, but I bet he's not losing any sleep. It is so unfair. Why God felt that I needed to experience that relationship is beyond my comprehension, but He brought me through it for a reason. I was just thankful that I didn't die at the hands of my ex. So there had to be a reason. I still haven't figured it out though.

I'm rushing because I am now an hour late for work. I quickly wash and moisturize my face, and brush my teeth. No time to take a shower; they'd better be happy I even showed up to work. I throw on some slacks and a cotton V-neck fitted shirt. I don't feel like putting on my heels right now, so I leave the house with my heels in my oversized pocketbook and wear my sneakers.

I get into my burgundy Avalon and notice that it is almost on empty. I convinced myself that I was too tired last night to go get gas. I planned on getting gas in the morning, because I didn't anticipate that I would be running late. When I pull up to the full service gas station, a young Hispanic looking guy asks if I will be paying with cash or credit. I hand him my credit card and tell him to put in forty bucks worth. The gas attendant finishes filling my tank and hands me the receipt to sign. I notice that he's looking at me kind of weird. I look up at him to ask what he's looking at, but he quickly looks away. I hand him the signed receipt and drive off.

As I am driving off, I notice something in my rearview mirror. It's my nose! When I put my moisturizer on this morning, I did it without looking and I had a ring of creamy white Cetaphil moisturizer around the inside of my nostril. I'm sure that's what the gas attendant was looking at. *Dang, he could have said something, instead of looking at me as if I had a third eye. I would have told him if something was on his face! Stupid ass! Good thing I found out it was there before I walked into work!*

I was so embarrassed! I try to look on the bright side. At least I didn't walk into work with cream in my nose. I'm not sure anyone at my job would feel comfortable enough to tell me. I never understood why some people felt that it was better to not tell someone that they had something on their face or in their nose in my case. Don't they realize that it is less embarrassing to hear it from someone early on in the day, than to interact with a bunch of people throughout the day and have nobody tell you?

When you find out for yourself, you take a mental note of all the people you came into contact with. It's awful. Why is it that not one person will tell you that you've got a booger hanging out or food in between your teeth when they see it? Instead they let you walk off to embarrass yourself with someone else. These are the same people that smile in your face and laugh at you behind your back. A real friend would tell you.

I finally get to work and I am in a bad mood, but I can't let them see that though; I fake the funk throughout the day. I work through lunch because I was late. All I want to do is finish up and go home; I usually enjoy coming to work, but after last night's nightmare, combined with my headache, I wanted to be at home.

As I am walking to the elevators, a new security guard decides to start up a conversation with me. I'm really not in the mood, so I answer his questions with short, one-word responses. Either he doesn't get the hint or doesn't care; he continues to pry. I finally figure out that he's trying to find out if I am single. He's a cutie, but I am not going to entertain dating someone that works with me. Although, I am now single, I still feel like Fritz is my man, so I politely tell him that I have a boyfriend and he backs off.

I really needed to talk to Fritz; I do want to spend my life with him; I just need him to give me a chance to explain that I wasn't rejecting him, I was rejecting the idea of marriage. I still have a lot of baggage and hang-ups from my last relationship. It's not as easy as just marrying someone because you love them; after all, I loved my ex and we were almost married and look how that turned out.

I thank God every day that he showed me the devil I was dealing with before we got married. If Fritz just hears me out, I think he'll come back to me. It's time for me to fix this; I think I will stop by his house this week after work sometime.

Charlene:

My wedding date is approaching and I'm starting to feel uneasy. I'm not sure why. I just feel like something is off or something is about to pop off. I've been in a down mood lately and I don't know why. I can't explain why I am feeling this way. I see no sense and telling anyone I am feeling this way.

Derek seems a little stressed too. He hasn't told me that he's stressed, but I can see it on his face. He hasn't asked to take me out anywhere lately; come to think of it, he hasn't even gone out lately. That includes spending time with me here. We've been talking on the phone more than we've been spending time with each other.

I haven't asked him to come over, but neither has he. Maybe he's getting cold feet. Maybe that's why I am feeling slightly depressed. I call Derek and ask if he wants to hang out tonight, because I'm feeling depressed. He said he had a lot of loose ends he needs to tie up. He suggested that I call Ava and Evelyn and hang out with them.

I didn't want to hang out with my girls. I wanted time with my future husband. Is this how it is gonna be? Is he gonna put me off on my friends when he doesn't feel like being my shoulder to lean and cry on? Something is not right in the universe; Something is up and I want to know what it is. God is trying to show me something, but I can't figure out what.

I hang up with Derek and I'm heated but, I don't call my girls; instead, I decide to kneel down and pray. I was taught to pray in times like these. I prayed for a half hour straight and by the time I was done praying, I felt better, but I was exhausted. My body decided for me to go to bed early. Tomorrow is going to be a better day; I am sure of it.

Ava:

That dog had a nerve to leave me a voice message telling me that I was to blame for him messing with that chick from Dorchester. *Who does that?* He said that he felt that he was no longer relevant in my life. He knew that I never needed him, but I never made him feel like he wasn't needed until a year ago.

A year ago, I became a manager at my job. According to this dog, I became more involved with my work than I was with our marriage. I get mad because he's not here for me to yell at him. I can't argue with a voice message. It was probably for the best, because I was ready to go off! He's about to get all of my attention now.

I made sure I saved the message and I will use it in court if needed. If Brian thought he saw my bad side before; he was wrong. Not only was he a jerk, but he was an arrogant jerk. He actually blamed me for his infidelity!

I changed all the locks after I asked him kindly to get the hell out. I took my money out of our joint account so that he couldn't live off my savings. He should have been looking for a job while he was on unemployment, instead of looking for ass. Now he can have that ass, with his broke ass.

I hope she can pay his bills, because I'm not. I took my engagement and wedding rings off and put them in a Ziploc plastic bag. I am going to pawn the rings or trade them up for something else. I no longer had a need for them. The more I think about what this man has done to my life, the angrier I become. He's going to cheat on me because I work too hard? That makes no sense at all.

Would he have liked it better if I was an underachiever and did the bare minimum? Better yet, how would he like it if I decided I didn't want to work at all? Then would he have decided to honor his vows and not cheat? Of course not, he would have cheated with someone that was ambitious. If a man is going to cheat he's going to cheat. There's no way around it and it usually has little to nothing to do with you.

I am angry and becoming bitter. Usually, I do a better job at dealing with my feelings. I was struggling with this and I decided that I was going to teach him a lesson. I couldn't wait on God to handle this one; I'm sure God has better things to do than to get involved with my drama. I looked up and said, "I got this one, God."

The next morning I drove to Dorchester. His car was exactly where I expected it to be, in front of his bitch's public housing building. It was early and the only people out were those that needed to walk their dogs before heading to work. Everyone else was either still sleep or getting ready for work.

I had plans for my soon to be ex-husband's car. I used my spare key and opened his door. Once inside, I took the egg salad that I prepared last night and smeared it all over his seats, head rest, radio, dashboard and under his floor mats. I left it out overnight, just to make sure the funk that I wanted to permeate did its job. By the time I was done, the car smelled like a huge fart.

I decided that since he'd made me angry, I was going to make sure he had something to be angry about too. His car will definitely have to be detailed to get rid of that mess I left. Over the next two weeks, I did things just to mess up his day.

I knew he had dry cleaning that he needed to pick up. I went to the dry cleaners and told them that I wanted to pay for my husband's bill. As I had hoped, they assumed that I was also picking up his clothing. I wasn't; I was only going to pay for my husband's bill.

The owner's wife was working today. She hung his suits on the rack for me to take. She then said that if I was all set, she had to go in the back to tend to something. When she left, I pulled out my scissors. I opened up the plastic dry cleaning bag and went to work on the crotches of his suits. It took me all of thirty seconds to ruin his suits. I closed the bag and then walked out of the dry cleaners, leaving his clothes behind.

Just as I was about to open the door to exit, the wife yelled that I forgot my husband's clothes. I told her that I only wanted to pay his balance. My husband would be back to pick them up later. It wasn't a lie. He'd arrive to find his bill already paid for by his loving, forgiving wife. Then when he goes to put on a suit, his dick will be hanging out of them. I figured that would be a suitable look for someone that doesn't know how to keep it in his pants.

After I did that, I decided to lay low for a while. I left him alone for two weeks. I figured that he would think I wasn't that angry anymore and he'd let his guard down. This is exactly what he did; once again, I took my anger out on his car. This time I did it late at night. During the two weeks that I called myself lying low, I collected my urine. Each day, I peed into an empty gallon water jug. I made sure I had two gallon's worth of pee to take with me.

Using my spare key, I opened his car door. The car smelled good. It smelled like it was just detailed. It's too bad for him that the next time he goes to detail his car, the detailers may turn his business down. I poured the urine on all of his seats and on his floor. *Try to get this smell out*. I also left his new girlfriend's sanitary wipes that were under my sink on the dashboard. Let him clean up this mess with them. *Shiiiiiit, he's lucky I didn't save my feces for two weeks*.

Charlene's wedding was soon and I honestly didn't think that I was going to be able to be in it. Both Brian and I were in the bridal party; we are supposed to walk together. I don't think that I could fake being cordial to him. In fact, I know I can't; I just might poison his meal. I need to call Charlene up and tell her that I wasn't going to be in her wedding.

Charlene:

Time just flew by. My wedding is next Friday, and my bachelorette party is this weekend; I can't wait. Ava did most of the planning, so I know it is going to be off the hook! She's an undercover freak; I can't imagine why Brian would ever cheat on her of all people. I'm sure his needs were being met. Why in the world would he stray? Men just don't know a good thing when they've got it. I guess that can apply to women too, because I really don't get Evelyn and her refusal to marry Fritz.

I really don't want any drama at my wedding. I am praying that there won't be any, but there is definitely the potential for some drama to occur. Derek asked Brian and Fritz to be his groomsmen. Of course, Ava and Evelyn are my bridesmaids. Since Ava and Brian have separated, Ava has been doing some cruel and unusual things to Brian.

Evelyn has been trying to get back in Fritz's good graces, but has been unsuccessful with reaching him. Last week, she even went by his house and waited for him in her car all night to come home. He never showed. After that she stopped trying, but I know she still wants him.

Everyone will be reunited for my wedding. I asked Ava and Evelyn to be on good behavior for the sake of my wedding and good pictures. They agreed that they would. I'm not that confident that they will keep their word. Ava's just so damn bitter and Evelyn is becoming obsessed with Fritz. I don't need them embarrassing me and ruining my wedding day.

I originally planned to have one hundred people at the wedding. That list grew to two hundred quickly. Derek just kept adding friends and family that he hasn't been in contact with in years. I really didn't see the logic in it. *Why invite people that haven't been a part of your life for a long time?* He was paying for half of it, so I really couldn't say much.

A call was left on my voice mail from the caterer. He didn't really say much except that he's been having a hard time reaching Derek. He asked that I tell Derek to return his call. I sure hope there's no issue with the meal we selected. Derek is in charge of this stuff. I gave him my half of the money. He said that he would take care of things so that I wouldn't have to stress myself out and worry. I was grateful that he offered to do that.

I don't want to know about the small stuff. I'll get a headache no matter how small of an issue it is. I texted Derek and told him about the caterer having a hard time reaching him and that he needed to call him. Derek texted me back that he would take care of it and not to worry, so I planned on doing just that . . . not worrying.

It's Saturday already; Ava and Evelyn gave me a spa gift certificate as a separate wedding gift. They said that it is their gift to me, but didn't want me to think that this gift was the main wedding gift. I would have loved it if they came with me to the spa, but they said that they still had some running around to do before the bachelorette party. We were supposed to meet at my house at 7 pm tonight. I can't wait.

Seven pm rolls around; Ava and Evelyn still aren't here, but I'm being patient. A minute later, I see Ava's Infiniti truck pull up. Evelyn and Ava beep the horn obnoxiously like they've lost their minds. I leave with my overnight bag in hand. I wasn't sure if I was going to return home tonight. My girls are in the car blasting Salt n Pepa's song "Get Up"! Ava had a new CD of old-school rap songs. I was definitely feeling it.

We drive to Jovan's in Rhode Island. Before we get out Ava, says "Tonight your name is Trina. Trina, here's your new platinum blonde wig." I look at her as if she's crazy when she hands me a short pageboy-styled blonde wig. She orders me to put it on. She also reminded me that I agreed to do what she said tonight. I agreed to give her full control of my night. She promised me that I would have a good time, so I did as I was told and put on my platinum blonde wig.

As I was doing that, Ava and Evelyn were putting on their wigs. We all had the same style wig, but we had different colors; Ava's was red and Evelyn's was pink. They are crazy. Needless to say we had a great time at the club. I used my new alias when guys approached me and I got more drinks that night than I ever had in the past; Ava was right, I had a good time. Changing my name to Trina and putting on the wig, made me feel like I was a different woman.

I was in a different state where nobody knew me. The men had no idea who I really was and that I was getting married next Friday. Ava gave me the gift of freedom. I was free to act however I wanted, I was free to act like a slut if I wanted. I was free to drink until I got tore up if I wanted. I was free to do whatever. There was no one there to judge me. "Weekend Charlene" was creeping back into the picture again.

Evelyn and Ava only had one drink. They said that they couldn't get tore up with me, because they were responsible for me. I appreciated that. I know that they wanted to drink. When I woke up the next morning; I didn't even know how I got home, but Ava and Evelyn were in my bedroom with me sleeping. I have great friends.

I barely remembered the night. I do know that I had a good time. When Evelyn woke up, she told me that I was the life of the party. I was dancing with all the guys. She said that we had to leave when I started strip teasing. My girls thought that I was just going to tease the men. Instead, I showed anyone who was watching, my braless boobs. They said that I kept yelling, "Trina Gone Wild!"

It was at that point that they took me home. I guess Trina was having too much fun. Who knew that a new wig and a new name could be so much fun! "Weekend Charlene" was back!

Ava:

It was fucking hilarious watching "Trina" last night. I told her that the wig was going to get her into trouble. When I told her that I might need to take the wig away from her, she sucked her teeth in the most ignorant way. This bi-polar broad told me that she was keeping her Trina wig. She planned to introduce Trina to Derek on their honeymoon. All I could do was laugh.

The grocery store was around the corner from Charlene's place. I tell the girls that I'll be back; I was going to buy some breakfast foods and let Evelyn cook for us. Evelyn sarcastically thanked me for letting her cook, with her smart ass.

I usually go to Market Basket near my house to grocery shop, but the closest one to Charlene's house is not close enough. I go to the supermarket around the corner from Charlene's, Super Stop and Shop. I don't frequent this supermarket so I had to actually read the signs in the aisles to find what I was looking for.

When I was done gathering our breakfast, I walked over to the check-out line. They were all long. None of the 12 items or less registers were manned, so I decided to go to the only self-check-out register that they had. There was one person in front of me. As she was taking her purchases from her basket, one of her items caught my attention. It was the same type of sanitary wipes that I found in my bathroom.

The sight of them brought back feelings of disgust and anger. The woman in front of me turned around to grab some gum. When she turned around, I thought I was seeing things. *Surely, this can't be the same woman that was up in my house giving head to my husband.* God was trying to tell me or show me something. Either way, I didn't have time to figure it out. My anger was building as each millisecond went by.

I decided it was time for this chick to feel some of my anger. She didn't even notice me, because I had on sunglasses. I let her finish checking out and I quickly checked my stuff out too. I only had a couple of items. Therefore, I was able to catch up to her in the parking lot; ironically, she was parked two cars away from me. I knew that the supermarket had security, so I had to be quick.

As she was putting groceries in her trunk, I slammed the trunk down. The bitch was quick and I just missed her hands. She turned around, looking all shocked and shit. Before the bitch could utter a word, I kicked her right in her coochie, like I was playing kick ball.

I know that shit hurt. She was in so much pain that she couldn't speak. She buckled at the knees and fell to the ground. I then hocked and spit on her, a nice, gooey loogie. I told her that if she reports this, the next time I see her, I won't be so nice. Then I casually walked back to my car and drove off with my heart racing!

When I got back to Charlene's, I told them everything that went down. Charlene said that I was lucky I wasn't arrested and Evelyn said that I could still get arrested; if she pressed charges. Evelyn wanted to know how I could kick someone in their coochie. I told her it was easy. I know that she'll think twice in the future before messing with a married man again. Both my girls thought that I was certifiably crazy, but Charlene was more worried about me being in jail for her wedding.

Evelyn:

The wedding is a couple of days away. I haven't seen Fritz since my birthday; I really miss him. I do realize that I let a good thing get away from me and I want him back. I thought about using desperate measures to get him back. I was thinking of telling him that I was pregnant with his baby and that's why I was calling him so much.

When I told crazy Ava what I planned on doing, she asked me what I was going to say when he found out that I wasn't really pregnant. I had a perfect excuse; I was going to tell him that I lost it due to the stress of possibly having a baby with a man that wouldn't even talk to me.

Ava told me that even she wouldn't go there. If he ever found out that I lied to him, it would destroy things between us forever. I thought of proposing to him at the reception; Ava thought that was a better idea, but Charlene might get mad at me for interfering with her day. I decided that I wasn't worried about Charlene. I was going to propose.

I know Fritz is a good man; at least, he's been consistently good to me. I should have never turned down his proposal. I can't see myself without him, and I pray he still feels the same way about me. I am going ring shopping.

I decide to go to the jewelry store where Derek's the manager. It's the middle of the day and not a lot of people are in the store. I scan the store and don't see Derek anywhere. I called Charlene earlier and I swore she told me that Derek was working today. I guess she had it wrong. Maybe he was on break.

A short, elderly, white lady with ostentatious jewelry and way too much make-up on greets me. She asks if she can be of any assistance.

"Is Derek working."

"No, he isn't. Is there something that I could help you with?"

"When will he be working again?" I say, without answering her question. With a slight hint of an attitude, she tells me that he won't be. I wasn't sure if she heard me wrong or if I heard her wrong. So, I asked her again. "What do you mean, he won't be?" She said that Derek stopped working for the store months ago. I could tell that I was working her nerves.

This is crazy, first Brian and now Derek. Maybe I need to find out if Fritz still has a job before I go proposing to him. I only went to Derek's store because he worked there. Other than that reason alone, I had no reason not to shop around. I thanked the woman and told her that I was window-shopping. Window-shopping meant that she wouldn't be making her sales goals today. She left me alone after I told her that.

I end up buying a platinum wedding band with three diamonds in the center. I figured I had to do just as good, if not better, than the ring he proposed to me with. Let's just say I had to go into my savings to pay for this ring; he is definitely worth it. I was getting excited and anxious.

After, I left the store; I went home to brainstorm on how I was going to pull this off. I came up with the idea of proposing to him, after I do the toast for Charlene and Derek. I started writing down my speech for the toast and my proposal. It had to be perfect. When I finished, I was proud of myself. I was a better writer than I thought; shoot, I should write speeches for the president. My cell phone rang while I was proofreading my speech. It was Charlene.

"Hello."

"Hey Evelyn."

"Hey girl. What's up?"

"I was wondering if you wanted to check out a movie tonight."

"Sure, I'm free. What did you want to see?"

"I was thinking of going to see Jason Statham's new movie. You know he's my favorite white man."

"You don't even know the name of the movie or what it's about, do you?"

"Nope," Charlene says, laughing.

"I'm glad you called, because I wanted to ask you how things were with you and Derek now that the wedding was approaching."

"Things are fine. Why do you ask?"

"No reason. I just wondered what it was like between couples a few days before they said I do."

"Actually we haven't seen that much of each other Evelyn, but we both are really busy."

"Well in a few days, you guys are going to be married and will be up under each other twenty-four seven."

Charlene nervously laughs and starts to talk about her favorite white man again. After ten minutes of debating over who is sexier; Jason Statham or my favorite white man Robin Thicke, we decide to meet at Showcase Cinemas in Revere.

I never brought up that I went to Derek's store and found out that he no longer worked there. That was his job to tell his fiancée that he quit. He knows Charlene told him that she is not going to marry him if he doesn't keep his job. Maybe he has a good explanation or another job. Who knows? I know that I was not going to be the one to break that to her. Next thing you know, I'll be blamed for their failed marriage.

After the movie, Charlene and I went our separate ways. She went home and I went to Ava's. I haven't spoken to Ava since she acted like a crazy person at the supermarket. It was time for a check in. When I arrived at her house, all of her lights were out except for her bedroom light. Her car wasn't there, so I didn't know what was up. I rang the doorbell anyway.

Ava, unlocked the door without opening it. She didn't say come in or anything. I opened the door and she was already headed upstairs. I figured something was up. So, I followed her upstairs to her bedroom. Ava got back in bed and didn't say anything to me. Either something was really wrong or she was being rude as hell. I walked over to the bed and asked what was going on with her. She said that someone named karma was messing with her, but her friend revenge was going to take care of that bitch. I told Ava to stop speaking in riddles and tell me what was going on.

When she turned around, I wanted to cry. Ava's face was all bruised up; her left eye was swollen shut and she had a cut that ran from her cheek to her chin.

"What the hell happened to you, Ava?"

"I told you that karma happened to me."

"What the hell is that supposed to mean?"

"It means what goes around comes around. Honestly, I'm okay."

"Well, you still haven't told me what happened."

Ava told me the story and I couldn't believe my ears. From my understanding, that chick that's messing with her soon to be ex-husband jumped her, with two of her friends. Ava was coming from the gym walking to her car and they jumped her. I asked Ava if anyone came to her rescue and she said that it was late, not a lot of people were even at the gym. I warned her about going to those 24-hour gyms.

Just because they were open for 24 hours didn't mean that she had to take advantage of their late hours. Nevertheless, she was walking back to her car and three women jumped her. She said that she didn't know what hit her. One of them hither in the back of the head. The other one kicked her in her back. She fell to the ground immediately. They punched her in the face with rings on.

That's how she got the cut that ran from her cheek to her chin. It lasted for under two minutes. She said that was the longest two minutes of her life. They stopped stomping her when she heard a man's voice say "that's enough." She knew that voice anywhere. It was Brian's. She could barely see through the one good eye that she had Left, because there was blood blurring her vision. She was able to see that it was Brian's car that they drove off in.

I told Ava that this was enough. All this vindictiveness had to stop. She could have been killed! Ava told me that they should have killed her because it was on now. I asked her what she meant by that. She said that she went to the police station and filed a report. Ava said that she told the police that Brian was angry about her divorcing him. The way she told it was that Brian waited for her to come out of the gym. He approached her asking to talk. When she wouldn't talk, he got angry and pinned her to the car; he forced her to listen. She couldn't go anywhere. She went as far to say that he slapped her a few times then pushed her to the ground. The next thing she knew, he was holding her down while his new girlfriend attacked her. Ava didn't even mention the two other girls. She filed a 209A and said that she was afraid for her life. She got a temporary restraining order against the both of them, because she said that they threatened to kill her.

That's not the worst of it. Before she filed the report, she drove to Craig's place and asked him to do her a favor. Craig looked at her and didn't even ask what happened. He told her no problem; Ava offered to pay him, but since she was family, he did it free of charge.

She gave him the spare key to Brian's truck. I didn't know that Ava could be so evil. I knew Craig could because he's been into all types of illegal things since we were teenagers. Ava had Craig arrange for Brian's new girlfriend to be gang raped. Ava said that since his new bitch liked the 3:1 ratio, referring to her getting jumped by three people, she thought it was only right that she return the favor. She arranged for three men to take their turn with her. Ava had truly lost her mind!

As for Brian, Craig had one of his flunkies put a loaded gun in Brian's glove compartment. A local detective owed Craig a favor, so Craig arranged for Brian to be stopped for a bogus traffic violation. When they run his plates, they will see that a warrant is out for his arrest. Then they will find a loaded gun that has a body on it in his glove compartment. Craig was so taken aback with the way that Ava looked that he threw some coke in the mix for good measure. I'm not talking about Coca-Cola.

When Brian got pulled over that same night, he was found with a loaded, unregistered, unlicensed gun, and enough coke in his glove compartment to look like he was distributing it. When Ava was done telling me the story, she said, "Checkmate." I couldn't believe that she went through such extremes to get back at a man that wasn't worth the time or energy she put into trying to hurt him.

This was a big deal. If Brian is arrested, he definitely wouldn't be in Charlene's wedding. With the way that Ava looks, I doubt she'll be in the wedding either. *Charlene is not going to believe this!* I decided to spend the night over Ava's and nurse her wounds. She needed serious counseling.

Ava:

Today was Charlene's wedding day. She's called me a thousand times since the Brian incident. I really didn't feel like talking. I was sure that Evelyn told her the entire story by now. I texted both of them and said that I will see them at the wedding and then I turned my phone off.

Luckily I was already on vacation from work. I originally planned to be spending the days leading to Charlene's wedding with Charlene, but that didn't happen. I was depressed; I couldn't understand how a man that vowed to honor and cherish me, could cheat on me. The same man could sit and watch me get beat down by the chick he was dicking down. He had become equivalent to the devil. I wanted him to die. He's turned my life upside down. I don't know who I am anymore. I have been thriving off punishing him. Who was I punishing really?

The truth is that I am hurting myself by becoming such a vengeful person; I used to consider myself a very forgiving person. Where that person went is beyond me.

I felt like God had forgotten about me. Where was God when Brian was cheating on me? What was God doing when Brian had me beat down? Haven't I been a good person? What have I done to deserve this? I wasn't the one that cheated. He was. Was I just supposed to turn a blind eye to it? Was I just supposed to forgive him and ask him to not do it again? What was I supposed to do?

I felt used, stupid, and dirty. I felt like the joke was on me. It wasn't a good feeling. I didn't know how to deal with these feelings. I never thought that it could happen to me. I know other wives got cheated on, but that couldn't happen with my husband. I gave him no reason to do this. If he could concoct a reason, I'd bet my life that it wouldn't be a good one.

I think about how his selfishness could have killed me. He could have slept with someone and passed on a disease that's life threatening. Men don't think about that. You are taking a big risk when you step outside of your marriage. Not only are you taking a risk, but your spouse is unknowingly taking the risk with you. I guess I'm lucky he gave me a curable STD.

I will never forgive him. I know my vows said for better or for worse, but I believe in divorce. Adultery is definitely divorce worthy. How could I stay with a man that would put my life at risk? How could I ever sleep with him again? I wouldn't trust him. I wouldn't be able to stop thinking about the other woman or women that he slept with. He would no longer be attractive to me. He'd have to rape me in order to get some.

I tried talking to women in the church, but I just kept getting the same crap for advice. They kept telling me that Jesus put up with way more than I have. If Jesus can forgive, so should I. Maybe they were right. Maybe I should be forgiving, but I'm not there yet. Call me a baby in Christ. I'm still on the milk and can't handle the meat.

It's two hours before the wedding and I am nowhere near ready. I thank God for small blessings because my eye went down dramatically. It was still black and blue, but I had some miracle foundation to cover that up. I missed my hair appointment. I was going to have to do it myself. I wondered who I would be walking with, because I had a restraining order out on Brian. If he showed up, you best believe I'd be calling the boys in blue.

I turned my phone on and I had a million messages. I couldn't be bothered with listening to them and I turned my phone back off. I was getting stressed just thinking about all of those messages; as far as I was concerned, they could all wait.

Charlene:

Today is supposed to be my wedding day, but I won't be getting married today. The caterer called and said that he has had a difficult time reaching Derek to pay the remaining balance. I asked how much was left. It couldn't be too much. He told me that half of the balance was still not paid. I immediately developed a lump in my throat. I could barely speak.

I asked the caterer to repeat what he'd just said. He told me that Derek has been promising to pay him and has asked for extensions. He said he'd extended it far enough. The caterer said that he didn't want to call me to worry me with this stuff, but he had no choice. Unless someone paid the remaining seven thousand dollars, there would be no caterer. I started to panic. I told the caterer that I had another account that should have that amount in there, and that I would make arrangements to get it to him. I asked him to give me thirty minutes and I would call him back.

Derek had a lot of explaining to do. Thank God, we had the rainy day account. I tried calling Derek several times after my phone call with the caterer. He never answered. I got in my car and drove to the bank. I filled out a withdrawal slip for eight thousand dollars. The way I estimated, we should have at least nine thousand dollars in it.

The bank teller started to process my withdrawal request and she started looking at the computer funny. She handed me back the withdrawal request and asked if I had the correct account number. She asked if I had another account. I told her that this was the only account that I had at this bank. The Eastern Bank teller looked at me sympathetically and told me that I didn't have enough funds in the account for that amount. I told her just give me seven thousand instead. The teller told me that I didn't even have seven hundred in the account.

My heart almost stopped beating. I told her that it had to be a mistake, because I gave my fiancé a thousand dollars two weeks ago to deposit. She showed me the balance on the account and I nearly passed out. I had one hundred and forty dollars in the account. I asked her to tell me the last time a deposit was made in the account.

I couldn't believe my ears when she said that the last time a deposit was made was over two months ago. I was ready to use the N-word and I don't use that word! *Derek better answer his damn phone!* I stormed out of the bank embarrassed as hell. I withdrew the rest of the money and closed the account. Not only did he not pay the rest of his portion of the bill, but he took all of our money out without my knowledge. What the hell was going on! I dialed the jewelry store to see if he got called into work today.

I felt like someone punched me in the gut. Derek no longer works there. I sent him a nasty text and told him that he better find his deceitful ass over to my house within the next hour. If he doesn't, there will not be a wedding tomorrow. An hour and a half later, Derek calls me and asks what's wrong. I thought he must have lost his mind.

"What's wrong baby?"

"What's wrong? What's right? Why hasn't the caterer been paid, and where is my rainy day money? Have you lost your mind? Do you know what type of day I've had?

"I can explain, Charlene."

"Please do; I am all ears. I can't wait to hear this."

"I'm going to pay you back all of your money."

"Why is my money gone, Derek?"

"I had to borrow it for something really important."

"If it was so important, why couldn't you tell me about it?"

"If I told you why I was borrowing it, I wasn't sure you'd approve. I was desperate."

"So what did you use my money for, Derek?" I say impatiently.

"Child support."

"I don't have time for games, Derek. You have to have a child to pay child support."

"I needed it for back pay of child support. They were going to take my license away."

"Okay, I must be missing something. When did you get a damn child?"

"I didn't want you to find out this way and I never knew how to bring it up."

"Bring up that you had child support payments or that you had a child, Derek?"

"Well both. This white girl swears up and down that her kid is mine. She even put my name on his birth certificate. I know she's lying. That kid could be anybody's kid. She's a hoe."

"So you mean to tell me that you have a child in this world that you are not taking care of? Some child that you played a part in making doesn't know his daddy?"

"I don't even know that he's my kid."

"How is that possible? Didn't you get a paternity test?"

"Yes. I got one."

"What did it say?"

"I don't know what it said. I never opened it. I knew that the kid wasn't mine."

"You mean you didn't open it, because you knew that the child was yours."

"I didn't need to open it. I told you she was a hoe. We slept together only a couple of times. She's been chasing me down for child support for the last four years now. You know Charlene, I'm glad that this is finally out in the open, because it was really stressing me out. Listen, I will pay you back the money that I borrowed and work everything out with the caterer."

"How are you going to do that, Derek?"

"Well I guess you know by now that I don't have a job, but I will get one soon and when I do I will give you all of my checks. This will all work out; just trust me."

I blacked out on him after that comment. Trust him! Was he crazy? I called him every derogatory name that I could think of. When he admitted that he left his jobs so often, because child support would catch up with him through his social security number, I thought that I would throw up in my mouth.

This fool kept quitting jobs because child support kept taking too much of his check. He decided that it wasn't worth working and getting half of his pay. He said when they threatened to suspend his license and issue possible jail time, he had no choice but to take my rainy day money.

I say *my* money because he put in less than ten percent of what was supposed to be in there. Not only was my husband-to-be a daddy, but he was also a thief. He basically stole my money to pay for his child support. He didn't pay the caterer because he didn't have it.

His checks in the beginning were good, but when child support started taking the money out he couldn't afford to contribute. He didn't know how to tell me this. After I finished cussing him out I hung up on him, but not before telling him to lose my number.

He called me back non-stop throughout the rest of the day. He called me again a few times this morning. I didn't know who to call; Ava wasn't herself lately and I just didn't feel right talking to her about it. Evelyn would have told me to forgive him and that's not what I wanted to hear. So I didn't call Evelyn. I couldn't call anyone else, because I felt like a fool.

Today there would be no wedding. They'll figure it out when I don't show. The caterer was very sympathetic and gave me back half of the deposit that I gave him for the food. I paid for the honeymoon; therefore, I was still going to Jamaica. I called my travel agent and basically told her that I wouldn't be going on a honeymoon, but I still wanted to go to Jamaica. She told me that she would transfer Derek's ticket into a credit and that she would cancel the reservations at the hotel that we were booked in. She found another hotel and rescheduled my flight for noon today.

I'll be on the flight to Jamaica by myself by noon. I needed this break; I really needed to re-evaluate my life. So that my girls and my family wouldn't worry, I decided to send them a text while I was at the airport getting ready to board. I told them that I was safe, but I would not be marrying Derek today or any other day. I let them know that I was going to Jamaica and would be back in less than two weeks. I asked them not to tell anyone else my whereabouts, especially not Derek. I didn't know what they were going to tell the guests that arrived at the wedding today, but I really couldn't worry myself with it.

Jamaica was beautiful. I arrived there feeling depressed and left feeling refreshed. I didn't speak to anyone from home while I was in Jamaica. I needed some "me" time. I got some "Weekend Charlene" time in while I was there. I refused to be on a tropical island talking to family and friends about the drama I left in Massachusetts. I just wanted to relax and think about my next move.

I even thought about moving. This warm weather had me feeling so good, that I thought it would be good for my mental health to move to a warmer climate. Warm weather certainly agreed with me. When I arrived back at Logan International Airport, I didn't bother to call anyone to pick me up; I took a cab home.

As I walked into my home, I saw my wedding dress hanging on the front of a closet door. I tried to convince myself that I was better off without him, but the truth was, even if I was better off without Derek, I still loved him. I was mad as hell at him, but the love button didn't just shut off. This was still fresh and the feelings of anger started turning into feelings of sadness.

Ava:

I arrived at the church and nobody has heard from Charlene. She's not at the church. She's not answering her phone. Her mother is in full panic mode. She finally gets ahold of Derek and finds out that they had a fight the day before. He hasn't heard from her since; Charlene's mom asks what the fight was about. She asked Derek if her daughter caught him cheating or something. He adamantly denied cheating.

Charlene's mom wasn't sure if she believed him. Nevertheless, she had not heard from Charlene; so she only had his word to go on. I checked my phone for messages and there were none from her. I was starting to get worried that something awful happened to her. Maybe she was in a car accident; I thought about calling the police, because there is no way she would miss her wedding.

Even if she did catch him cheating, she would still show up for the wedding. She would show up to cuss him out in front of everyone even if she didn't plan on marrying him. This was definitely out of character for her. When she wasn't there by the time the wedding was supposed to start, I knew she wasn't coming. Charlene was punctual, responsible, and considerate. This was so unlike Charlene.

Something was up. I walked over to Derek and told him to save the bullshit for Charlene's mom. Tell me where the hell my girl was and why this wedding wasn't about to take place. Derek told me the same story he told Charlene's mom, but he told me that he kept a secret from Charlene. The secret is the reason why she's not here today. He was surprised that she hadn't told me; quite frankly, so was I.

Once Charlene's mom addressed the wedding guests and basically cancelled the wedding on Charlene and Derek's behalf, I packed my stuff and headed back home. Evelyn, was crying as if it was her wedding that got cancelled. We barely spoke.

Evelyn:

My plans were ruined. Charlene was a no-show for her own wedding. Of course, Derek had something to do with it, but he was being tight-lipped with the information. Fritz arrived, but went straight to the men's dressing room and never came out. I think once he found out there would be no wedding, he left out the back door. I never got a chance to propose to him.

When I got home, I texted Fritz and said that I know that he's upset and hurt because of me. I told him that I am very sorry. I asked him to call me back so that we could talk, I told him that I loved him and that I am miserable without him. Surprisingly he called me back. We talked for two hours straight and then he said he had to take care of some things.

During this call, I found out that Fritz had been going through something life-altering. Fritz was sick. He didn't have cancer, but he had a disease that could only be treated and not cured. Ignorant I started wondering if it was contagious and if he gave it to me. I later learned that it was a genetic disease and I couldn't catch it from him.

I had never heard of this disease. At first, I thought that he was playing or just trying to push me away. Fritz has Fabry disease. I asked him what happens to people with Fabry disease. He told me that for some men that go untreated, the life expectancy is forty years old. He said with treatment, his life would be prolonged. I couldn't believe my ears. Fritz wasn't forty, but he wasn't a decade away from it.

I wanted to know more about the disease. Fritz just told me that he was missing an enzyme and as a result, some of his vital organs were or could be affected. I asked him how he found out that he had it. He told me that he went for his eye exam the day after my birthday and the ophthalmologist found whorl-like pattern in his eye. This was a symptom of Fabry disease; further testing confirmed the diagnosis.

He starts his first treatment on Monday. I wanted to offer to be there for him, but something made me hold back. I was so gung ho about marrying this man. I was uncomfortable with how I was feeling about him now. Should I love him any less now that I know he has a disease? Do I want him any less now that I know he has a disease? I needed to answer a couple of questions before I started full speed ahead with Fritz.

I didn't end up going to Fritz's first treatment. He told me that he expected to be there for at least four hours. He took the entire day off from work. I couldn't imagine why he would be there for so many hours. I didn't want to be there for my entire day. I didn't offer to go with him. I felt bad, but I still had some things that I needed to think about. I still had some research to do about Fabry disease.

It really made me re-evaluate my feelings for Fritz. Could I love him with this disease? I told Fritz that I would check on him. He seemed grateful, but I felt guilty. My heart said that I should have agreed to go with him to his first treatment. The selfish part of me didn't want to watch him get an intravenous infusion like a cancer patient. For better or for worse, was I ready for that level of commitment?

When I checked in on Fritz, he said that he was really tired and wasn't really up to conversing; I felt dismissed. I told him that I understood and would check on him again tomorrow. I never did call him the next day. It wasn't until the following week that I called him again. By then, I did my research. I found out everything that I needed to about the disease. I made my decision. I would pursue a life-long relationship with Fritz.

I didn't realize it, but I have been giving my ex-fiancé power, even after I left him. It was time for me to take my power back and get my man back. The question that remained unanswered was would he pursue a life-long relationship with me.

I found out the answer to that question when I showed up at Fritz's next infusion appointment. It was exactly two weeks from the first infusion he received. I asked him to marry me right before they put the needle in his arm. I got down on both knees and presented him with the ring I bought.

He was speechless and I was nervous. I knew that I had hurt him deeply. I knew that I didn't deserve him, but I wanted him. I needed him. I loved him more than he knew. He looked at the ring and a tear came down his cheek when he read the inscription. The inscription read: For better or Fabry.

The infusion nurses were so excited for us. They said that they have never witnessed a proposal at the infusion site. They thought that my inscription was clever and thoughtful. I told them that they were all invited to our wedding; I wasn't waiting. I told him that I wanted to get married in three months or less.

He thought that I was crazy. He told me that he wasn't dying; we didn't need to rush. I told him that we should have been married a long time ago and I didn't want to keep him waiting anymore. We compromised and decided to get married in six months.

Ava:

Evelyn called me and told me that she proposed to Fritz and he accepted. I congratulated her. She told me that the wedding was in six months. She asked me if I would be a bridesmaid. I told her that the last wedding I was in never happened. I asked if she was sure that she wanted me in it.

Evelyn told me that her wedding is not going to be cancelled. I was happy for her. She finally put her fears on the back burner. She was finally going to marry the best man that she's ever had. Fritz is a good man. He is nothing like her ex. She has nothing to worry about; they are a good match.

She told me about his disease. I had never heard of Fabry disease. She told me that he was missing an enzyme and some of his vital organs like his heart and kidney could or would be affected due to this missing enzyme. I asked if there is a cure, and she told me no.

Fritz is on some type of treatment that requires him to have an infusion every two weeks for the rest of his life. I asked Evelyn what she thought about him having this disease. She said that she didn't love him any less. She said that she did take some time to think about it. She questioned if she really wanted a relationship with him forever.

She said that she came to the conclusion quite simply. She loved him and still wanted to spend the rest of her life with him, despite the disease. She has always loved him; she never accepted his proposal because that's when everything got out of hand with her ex. She didn't want her relationship with Fritz to change.

In her mind if they never got engaged, things would never change for the worse. She sees now that she was just being stupid and almost lost the love of her life thinking that way. I was impressed. I was also a little jealous. Evelyn had a great man. He was loyal, attentive, generous and very good-looking. Why couldn't my husband have been more like Fritz?

Why was I going through this drama with my soon to be ex-husband? Why did I get the cheating husband? What did I do to deserve a man like Brian? Tomorrow is my court hearing. My restraining order was only for ten days and then I had to go to court to get it extended for another year. I was debating if I wanted to show up; I just wanted nothing more to do with him.

Was I really afraid of Brian or his girlfriend? No, I wasn't. Did he deserve to be in jail? Yes, he did. I felt like there should be a prison for cheating husbands. I'd love to be the warden of that facility. I'd hire Lorena Bobbitt to provide mandatory sensitivity training. They would return to the community as reformed men. The chances of recidivism would be slim to none.

After having a long talk with myself, I decided not to go to court to extend the restraining order. I started feeling remorseful; I didn't have to behave as evil as Brian had. I'm really not that type of person to be so vindictive, but I guess you never know what you will do if you are pushed to your limit.

I just wanted all of this madness to end. I was tired of the back and forth. I was tired of trying to teach him a lesson. What lesson was God trying to teach me? I wondered what all of my suffering was for.

At some point, I had to stop feeling sorry for myself. Life was ten percent of what happened to you and ninety percent of how you respond to it. At least, that's what my pastor said. I needed to work on my ninety percent in a big way. I didn't like how my life was turning out. I had the power to change my life. I needed to leave the pity party and start making some changes.

ONE YEAR LATER

Ava:

I don't know why divorces take so long to finalize, but I am officially divorced from Brian. I thought about changing my last name back to my maiden name, but I ended up keeping it the same. I built a life around the name Ava Ford. I want nothing to do with him, but I am keeping his last name.

I heard that the girl he left me for is pregnant. Good for them; I thank God that I didn't have a child with this man. If I did, I would still have to be in contact with him on some level for the sake of the child for the rest of my life. The rest of my life is a long ass time.

Brian only served six months in a correctional facility. The gun charge didn't stick, but the possession of narcotics charge did. I ran into him at the mall a week after he got released. I must say, he looked real good. He definitely spent his time working out. Why was he in a jewelry store? When I entered the store, my intent was to approach him to say a few words. Before I got to him, however, his pregnant whore came over to him and started tongue-kissing him.

Instead of Brian concentrating on the kiss, he had his eyes locked on me. He looked at me as if he wanted to slap the shit out of me. The bold part of me started to walk over to him and dare him, but I had more sense than that. When I noticed that he had his middle finger up at me, I rolled my eyes at him and walked away. I heard the words, "Bum Ass Bitch," being said as I exited the jewelry store. I turned around as if I was gonna do something; I then laughed and headed back out of the store.

Life has been so peaceful since Brian and I split up; I didn't realize how much of myself I lost being in that marriage with him. The first year of marriage was good. Everything after that year sucked. Brian and I still can't have a civil conversation. If we could, I would ask him when in the relationship did he start feeling unfulfilled? At what point did I lose him? I lost him way before he started sleeping with his new girlfriend. At what point did he start feeling unhappy with me? That would be when I lost him.

I realized that I stopped loving him before I found him with that girl in the shower. Brian never did more than his fair share and that caused me to resent him. On top of that, Brian walked and talked like everyone owed him something. He had an air of entitlement about him; I made the mistake and confused that with confidence. I am better off without him. There was no doubt in my mind that I could and would do better.

As of right now, I am not seeing anyone. I have been on a few dates, but nothing to write home about. I've been thinking about jumping the color border and opening my mind to the possibility of finding love from someone other than a black man. I never thought that I would say that, but there it is.

Don't get me wrong, I still love and prefer black men. I have just decided that it doesn't have to start and end with them. I can see myself with a white man. He'd be the type of man that has Jason Statham's swagger, Hugh Jackman's body and Michael Phelps's height. He's that Olympic swimmer that smokes weed. He'd also have Daniel Craig's sex appeal. That's my type of white man. Now where is he hiding?

Who am I kidding? If I found him, he wouldn't want me. I've definitely fallen off. I'm a solid size twelve. I have grown a gut that I didn't have a year ago. Every time I take my pants off, I have a red ring around my stomach. That's from my fat hanging over when I sit down. I have dents and bullet holes in places I have never had before. My arms are no longer defined. My armpits now have fat seeping out. There's no way that any man would want me.

I have a whole lot of working out to do before I'd catch the eye of anyone worthy. On my to-do list today is finding a gym to join. Not only am I going to join a gym, but I plan on going at least three times a week. I'm going to get down to at least a size eight within four months. I got a whole lot of sit ups, crunches, squats and arm curls to do. Don't get me wrong; I am still fly, but I'm not at my flyest.

I told myself that I am not even going to go shopping, because I don't plan on being this size very long. This is serious business; I can't let my marketable years go to waste. After I go join the gym today, I am going to head into Boston and make an appointment to have my hair braided. This way, I won't worry about sweating my hair out. That used to be one of my biggest excuses for not working out.

I really don't feel like sitting anywhere for half of a day, but it's worth it. I think I might get some light blonde pieces of hair mixed in with the dark brown new growth that I have. That's definitely not something I would normally do, but these aren't normal circumstances.

You can't expect change if you won't change. I'm all about change this year; I've been going to church more often. I'd stopped going when I found Brian with that girl. I felt like God just forgot about little old me. I see now that he hasn't and didn't back then. I was too busy fellowshipping with the devil to realize that God was there all the time. Church has been good for me. I'm not as bitter as I was before; I can honestly say that I have forgiven Brian. I haven't told him that, but I have.

When I arrive into Dorchester, I realize that it's the day that Ashmont Hills has their annual yard sale. I drive down to Alban Street. One of my home girls is selling all of her good shit from Pottery Barn. People think that I only like expensive things. They definitely have it twisted; I like quality things, but I like a bargain just like the next person.

Monique sold me about eight hundred dollars' worth of stuff for my home for two hundred dollars. None of the stuff looked used. She's not fooling me; I know this shit is hot. She must have a booster or has a hookup with someone that actually works there. Did I care that my purchases were probably stolen? Not in the least! Next stop will be to Joe's in Dudley to get their addictive steak and cheese. Then I will swoop over to Frugal Bookstore in Roxbury to pick up a few black books to read. I don't know when I'll make it to the hairdresser to set up an appointment; maybe, I'll just call.

Evelyn:

I've been married for six months to Fritz and life has been extremely trying. I want to work on starting a family and he's scared that he'll pass on the disease if we have a girl. I told him that we may have a boy. He says that he doesn't want to chance it; I remind him that before we got married he said that he wanted to start a family with me.

In fact, he said he wanted a big family. His response to that is that was he felt that way before he knew he had Fabry disease. I want a child. If we have a girl, we will get her on therapy as soon as she develops any symptoms. If we have a boy, then, we won't have to worry about the disease, because fathers can't pass it to their sons. It has something to do with the X chromosome. Regardless, I want a child.

Fritz isn't being agreeable. It's gotten to the point that I wonder if I made a mistake. Fritz knew that I wanted children before we got married. He knew that he told me he wanted a big family. Why would he think it would be okay to go back on something that important? I stopped taking my birth control. I'm not sure how nosey he is so, I still refill my prescription and flush a pill each morning.

We are going to have a baby; he can't let his fear of having a child with a disease stop us from having a family. Once I am pregnant, he'll be so happy that he'll forget about his fears. If not, it will be too late. The baby will not be aborted.

I feel a little scandalous for not taking my birth control and not letting him know about it. He doesn't understand that I am not getting any younger. My eggs are getting older; shoot, I recently found a gray hair down there and it was not pretty. If all goes well, I will find out if I am pregnant or not tomorrow. Tomorrow will make me be one week late; I have not gotten my period. I'm not going to waste my time with the home pregnancy tests. I already made myself an appointment with my OB/GYN. My appointment is first thing in the morning; I am so anxious and I have nobody to talk to about this. I'm too embarrassed to call anyone. Who wants to share that they had to deceive their husband in order to get pregnant? I feel like one of those young girls trying to trap their boyfriend.

Fritz is supposed to be taking me to dinner. He said that something good happened to him at work and he wanted to share the news with me over dinner tonight. Well, I have some news for him too. I went to the doctor and I am pregnant. I am so happy, I have been smiling since I walked out of the doctor's office this morning. I was going to tell Fritz when I spoke to him on the phone, but he was so excited about him having good news for me, I figured I'd save my news until later.

I arrived at the restaurant early. Instead of going home and changing; I decided that I'd just have dinner in my work clothes. My outfit was nice enough to go to dinner in. I had so much anxiety, I ordered a rum and Coke. I gulped it down before I realized what I'd just done. I was there to tell him about my pregnancy and there I was drinking alcohol. Pregnancy wasn't going to be easy for me, because I like to have a drink every now and again and not just wine.

I had the waiter take the evidence away and bring me an iced tea. Fritz was already going to be worried about us possibly having a child with Fabry disease. I didn't want him worrying about me giving our child fetal alcohol syndrome too. It was now six pm and Fritz was finally walking through the front entrance. I waved him over to our table and put on my biggest grin. As soon as he took off his coat and sat down, I asked him to tell me his good news. I told him that I also had some good news for him.

He decided that his news could wait. He asked me what has me grinning like a Cheshire cat. I told him that my news could wait. I urged Fritz to go first; I figured that my news was going to be bigger than his so it was best to save it for last.

"I got a promotion."

"That's great, Fritz!"

"I know! I worked my butt off for these last eight months, hoping that they'd notice."

"So tell me more about your position."

"I'd basically be a regional manager. I'm so excited. This is such a great opportunity."

"Well, I'm happy for you. With promotions come raises. Did you get a raise?"

"Yes Evelyn, I got a thirty-thousand dollar raise!"

"What? That's great Fritz!"

"I know, I know. I almost can't believe it. I haven't told you the best part."

"What could be better than a promotion and a raise?"

"We are moving to California. I am the new West Coast regional manager!"

"How could you accept a position all the way on the other side of the country and not consult me first? That is so selfish of you. Did you think that I would want to leave my friends and family and move to California? We've been married for six months and here you go making huge decisions for the both of us, without even running it by me."

I grabbed my tea and sipped it. "You had to know before today that the job was in California. I know you. You are not one to skip the specifics. Why didn't you tell me before that if you got the promotion we would be relocating? Why did you fail to mention that part? I can't believe this shit!" I yell as the waiter approaches. I give him a dirty look and he turns back around and checks in on the next table.

"Evelyn, you are making a bigger deal out of this than it really is."

"Oh well, I'm glad you think life-changing decisions are no big deal, because I got some life-changing news for you. I'm pregnant and I am not moving to California."

Charlene:

A month after I got back from Jamaica, I started seeing Derek again. What I should say is I secretly started seeing him again. None of my family or friends were aware. Today would mark our one-year anniversary if we'd gotten married. I am really not sure why I am still dealing with him.

I told myself at first that I wasn't really seeing him, I was just sleeping with him every now and then. Every now and then has turned into a few times a week. He's here so much that he may as well live here. In fact, he's asked me if he can move in. Of course, I told him no. I tell him that we are not back together and that we aren't exclusive. He doesn't believe me though. He says okay, but I know he thinks I am only fooling myself. I don't date anyone else. I give him all of my free time. Things are almost the same way they were when we were engaged. Why would he believe me? I barely believe me.

It's been really difficult hiding my relationship with Derek from my friends and family. Just so I don't have to answer too many questions, I find myself distancing myself from them. They think that I'm depressed on some level. I've tried to convince them that I'm not, but I realized that it is easier to let them believe that I'm stressed than to admit that I went back to Derek.

Since last year, Derek has admitted that he did look at the paternity test. It proved that he was the dad; he just couldn't handle the truth, so he denied it. Derek has been paying child support faithfully since he borrowed that money from me. I've asked him when he was going to start paying me back and he always gives one excuse or another. I know that I'm not getting that money back. He'd have to rob a bank to get me all my money back. He could at least make an effort to do so by paying me in installments.

I know that I need to leave him alone. Just the fact that I hide him from friends and family is a clue that us being together is not good. Every other day, I am telling myself that I'm going to stop dealing with him. It's as if I'm addicted to him.

Just like sweets, we get addicted to them and know that they are no good for us. There is no nutritional value, but we still find ourselves eating them. They make us fat, yet we still can't let go. Each time we try, the diet is short lived. We feel guilty each time we go back to the sweets, but not guilty enough to leave them alone.

I miss my family and friends. Life with Derek isn't worth losing them. He is starting to grow up, but not to the level that I would need to have a relationship with him. I've decided that I am going to tell Derek that I don't ever see us having a future together. I will tell him that I can no longer do whatever it is we are doing. I will cut things off for good. He'll be over tonight after work. I will cut our ties then.

I have all of his things in a small garbage bag, ready to go. There wasn't much to pack. He just had some toiletries and a change of clothes. I never let him leave too many personal items here. I was fearful of having too much evidence of him being here in case someone came to visit.

Derek showed up much later than expected. He said that he was coming after work, but then he didn't show until close to ten pm. By that time I was livid. I planned on being cordial, but the later it got, the more pissed I became. He acted as if I didn't have a life and would just wait on him. He made a good point. That's exactly what I've done in the past and exactly what I did tonight. The difference with tonight is that this will be the last night that I wait on him. He's out of my life for good this time. No revolving doors are installed at my house. He and I are through!

The next morning, as I'm on my way to work, I get a call from my friend that now lives in North Carolina. She said that they laid her off from work yesterday. She was pissed because they had the nerve to do it at the end of the day; I felt so bad for her. She just got out there six months ago. She has no family out there. She was brave enough to take a chance and get out of Boston to start a new life in Charlotte. She never expected her job to lay her off six months after she got there.

I silently said a prayer to God. I thanked Him for keeping a roof over my head, food in my stomach and a paycheck in my bank account every two weeks. Here I was, getting depressed over my love life and my friend didn't know where her next check was coming from.

Ava:

I went to the gym strong for about four days, and then I fell off. I stopped going. One day it was because it was raining, the next day it was because it was cold out. The day after that, it was because I was getting my period. Then after that, I just didn't feel like it. It is no surprise that I've gained more weight. I'm now in a size fourteen. I have a slight double chin and I need to go up a size in underwear. Even my coochie has gained weight! Nobody besides my GYN will be down there anytime soon. So I guess I have nothing to worry about.

My cute athletic build has turned into a thick frame. It was not a good look for me. I've eaten an entire bag of potato chips and finished an entire two-liter bottle of soda. I feel like a whale, but that didn't stop me from eating some ice cream thirty minutes after I finished the chips. I'll admit it, I'm addicted to junk food. I've always liked junk food, but I was active before. I was burning more calories a year ago.

I remember when I started to gain weight in junior high school. Instead of my mom telling me to stop eating so much junk food, she took the direct approach. Her words were, "Bitch, you are getting fat." She didn't yell at me. She just walked by me and mentioned it casually.

My mother is a size six. Today, she wouldn't even recognize me if she walked past me. I'd hit double digits and that was unacceptable in her eyes. When Evelyn started gaining weight in high school, she complained that her mom was too passive aggressive. Evelyn's mom handled her delicately. She told her about new diets she heard about on talk shows. She bought her exercise DVDs. She even bought her fat-free snacks in bulk. Evelyn said that she would have preferred if her mom just said, "Bitch, lose some weight."

I don't look in the full-length mirror anymore. When I do look in the mirror, it's from the neck up. I know what I look like neck down; I look big. I ask myself, "How did I get here?" I'm asking myself this while I'm pulling up to McDonald's drive-through. I order two double cheeseburgers and a large order of fries. I feel guilty and order myself a diet soda. I tell myself that I will eat a salad tonight for dinner and workout to one of my many exercise DVDs.

When I get home later that day, I go straight to the refrigerator to make a salad. The lettuce I have in the refrigerator is old and the tomatoes are moldy. I lose my appetite for about five seconds, and then I decided on eating a couple of large bowls of Fruit Loops for dinner. The exercise DVD never got turned on. I went right to bed after eating; I didn't wash my face or brush my teeth, I just didn't care anymore.

I was depressed; I knew it, but it was hard to admit it. My life had changed, my friendships had changed, my marital status had changed and my weight had changed. Life was just a big bowl of change. It was hard for me to transition smoothly into this involuntary change; I didn't know what to do with myself. Despite all of the change, I still had a lot going for me; I had a lot to be grateful for.

I listened to the radio and heard a story on NPR about a village in Africa being slaughtered. Women and children weren't spared. They were mutilated and raped. They were defenseless. The corruption ran deep; so deep that they couldn't turn to the police, because they were a part of the corruption. It really put things in perspective. After listening to that horrific story, I realized God was trying to really show me how good I have it. Things could always get worse. I was ready for things to get better, not worse.

Charlene:

I decided that I needed to get Derek out of my system and someone else into it, if you know what I mean. I decided that it was time to harness some of that free spirit that "Trina" had. I wasn't about to go "Weekend Charlene" crazy, but I was going to lighten up a little bit and choose what rules I was going to follow going forward. I was going to do things outside of the box. I wasn't always going to do what people expected Charlene to do.

The first thing on my agenda was to start dating. I was going to start dating men and not with the intention of making them my next husband. I was going to just go out and have a good time. I planned on dating all types of men, all colors and all professions; I would not limit myself. Nathaniel is going to be first on my list.

He's been trying to persuade me to the other side for quite some time now. I never entertained it. Today was a brand new day. The next time Nathaniel Gregory asked me out on a date I would accept. I just might ask him out myself, with his sexy white self.

It was time for a change. I wasn't sure what I wanted to do with my hair just yet. So I decided to go to a wig shop and try on different wig styles. I decided that I liked the "Trina" wig the best. I went out the next day and got my hair cut in a blunt bob cut with straight bangs. I looked like a black China doll when I left the salon. I looked damn good. It was quite a change for me.

Two blocks up the street was a Talbots. I walked right past it. I went into a boutique, and bought the sexiest dress they had. My date with Nate was tonight. I'm not sure if he has ever dated a black woman, but if this was his first time, I was going to give him a glimpse of what he's been missing with the sisters.

I took a few days off from work this week. Nate didn't have the opportunity to see my new hair cut at work. Although, Nate and I didn't work in the same department; we worked for the same company and saw each other in meetings often.

We agreed to meet at a restaurant in Boston. The plan was to have dinner and then go to a comedy show playing at the Wilbur Theatre. I was surprised that he had tickets to see Gary Owen. I didn't even know that he knew who Gary was. All eyes were on me when I walked into the restaurant.

The females were hating because I looked good and wasn't holding my stomach in. The men were drooling because my dress accentuated every good asset I had. I've always been good-looking, but this dress and new hairdo took me to another level. I looked sexy and seductive. My make-up was flawless and I smelled delicious.

When I walked toward Nate, I know he didn't recognize me, but he was mesmerized by my new swagger. Once I stopped at his table, all the men in the place were envious. Most of them were black; Nate was the only white guy in the restaurant besides one of the waiters. He wasn't hard to find. When I stood in front of him, I swear I saw his penis jump. I acted as if I didn't see it and asked if he was going to pull out my chair or have me stand there all night. The night went better than expected. We had a great dinner and the comedy show was hilarious!

Nate was a perfect gentleman. I was feeling a little frisky, so I let him slip me a little tongue when he kissed me good night. He tried to graze my booty, but I didn't let him. We had to leave something for the next date. There would definitely be another date. I never thought I would date a white guy, but Nate had me thinking anything was possible. It was nice to go on a date with someone who picked up the tab. That wasn't the case with Derek.

Evelyn:

The man that vowed to love me for better or for worse threatened to walk out on me, after I gave him the news about the pregnancy. He had the nerve to ask was the baby his; I couldn't believe my ears. Of course the baby was his. He said that he had to ask because it was his understanding that I was on birth control pills and that I took them regularly.

I told him that the pill isn't a hundred percent foolproof. He said that he can't prove it, but he wouldn't put it past me to have purposely missed a pill here and there. I told him that I was offended and this was not the reaction that I expected my husband to have when I told him about my pregnancy.

He said that he knew I was lying. At that point, I confessed and then I flipped it. I told him that it's pathetic that I had to go through such measures to start a family with my husband. I emphasized the word husband. He told me that since I decided to start a family without his consent, he was moving his family to California without my consent.

He must have lost his mind. He told me that if I didn't want to go, I could stay here, move in with my mother, and raise the child with her. I said nothing. I was in awe. Fritz never spoke to me this way or treated me this way; I felt like telling him to kiss my black ass, but I had to think things through. Did I want to raise this child without his daddy? Fritz is a good man, but now I question if he would be a good daddy.

What if we had a girl? Would he turn his back on the baby? Fritz has turned into a man that I barely recognize. I know that he has a life-threatening disease, but he should be grateful there is a treatment out there for it and thank God for each day he gives him. He's become such an unpleasant person to be around. Maybe he *should* move to California without me. Lord knows that I don't want to move on the other side of the country and have to deal with his moody behind.

I'm going to sleep on it, but I really don't appreciate him giving me an ultimatum. I don't like that he thinks he can boss me around. Who does he think I am? I'm his wife, not his kid; he needs to act like he he's aware of that.

I knew things would change once we got married. The same man that begged me to marry him is acting as if he doesn't want to be married. He can't think that he'll be married long behaving like that. The crazy man before him thought he was going to run my life; I will not let Fritz turn into my ex. If he does, I won't be sticking around.

Ava:

Okay, enough is enough. I need my life back. I have about four weeks of vacation time saved up and I'm going to take it. I'm not going to take it and just sit at home. I'm going to spend my time getting reacquainted with the gym and church. My life has changed for the worst since I've stopped going to both of those places.

Those places are the places where I always felt good after leaving them. I needed to start doing things that make me feel good. I signed up for a personal trainer and I asked for the toughest one they had. I needed my figure back. I feel like I lost a part of me when I lost my physique; this size fourteen has got to go. No more miss piggy panties for me; I wanted my Scandalous Panties by Tracey Cooper to fit.

Once I got back from church on Sunday, I felt so uplifted. I promised myself that I would go to Bible study during the week. I didn't make that promise to anyone else, just in case I didn't make it. I got out of my church clothes and changed into my gym clothes. I had an appointment with my new trainer in thirty minutes. The gym wasn't that far from my house, so I had plenty of time to change and make it there in time.

I arrive at the gym. I walk to the front desk and tell them that I have an appointment with Lance. They told me to sit tight. He will be right with me. As I waited, I decided to sip on my Gatorade. Lance walks up to me while I'm swallowing my drink. I only know his name because he is wearing a nametag. He says to me "I suuuuure hope that tastes good, because that is the last one you will have. From here on out honey; its water, water, water!"

I'm slightly embarrassed, because he was extra loud and people were staring. I figured that it was a good idea to put the drink back in my bag. As soon as I attempted to, Lance reached for it. He took it from me and threw it in the trash. I wanted to cuss his behind out for being so damn rude, but I didn't. I'd just come from church and didn't want to backslide that quickly.

Come to find out, Lance is a great trainer. He worked me out five days a week for three weeks straight. My old figure was trying its best to come back. Lance not only trained my body, but he trained my mind. Between Lance and church, my self-esteem was becoming more and more positive. Lance is the ideal man; he is smart, physically fit, spiritual, good-looking and single.

After the first week of working out, I felt like I'd known him for years. We both shared our history. It felt so easy and natural opening up to him. I jokingly asked him where he'd been all my life. He told me that it was too bad I was a woman, or else I would have been the perfect man for him. I couldn't help but crack up. He liked dick just as much as I did.

It took hard work and discipline, but Lance had me down to a size ten after three and a half weeks. By then end of next month, I should be back to my old size. My body was feeling good and church had my soul feeling good. Bible study has been so fulfilling. I wanted to share everything I learned with whoever would listen. Four weeks ago I was a different woman. I was fat and depressed. Today, I'm slimmer and truly happy.

Lance has provided me with a work out session and a therapy session combined. He has no idea what a blessing he has been to me. I want to do something special for him; but I just wasn't sure what to do to show my appreciation for my new BFF.

I decided to buy him something. After Bible study, I am going to head to the Coach store. I know Lance wanted a new Louis messenger bag, but he was going to have to settle for a Coach one. His next man was gonna have to buy him that.

I met a man at Bible study tonight. His name is Tim. He's from out-of-state and was looking for a church home. He said he joined the church a month ago, but had to leave to tend to an ill parent. He was gone for almost a month. I wondered why I hadn't seen him. Long story short, he asked me for my number and I gave it to him. He said that he would call me this evening; we will see if he is a man of his word. In the meantime, I'm off to buy that Coach messenger bag for my new BFF.

I went into the store only for Lance's bag. I came out of the store with his bag plus a pair of casual Coach sneakers, a scarf, and a wallet for me. After I left the store, I almost turned around and walked right back in to return all the stuff that I got for myself. Then I heard Lance's voice in the back of my head saying, "Bitch, you deserve it and much more." He told me that if I didn't believe it, nobody else would; I agree with him.

Brian almost had me believing that I was only worth going Dutch. I took off my flip-flops and put on my new Coach sneakers before driving off. On my way home, I got an urge to stop by McDonald's and get some fries. I looked down at my stomach and was grateful it no longer obstructed my view to my coochie. McDonald's fries was not worth a fat belly.

When I got home, I looked at my cell and saw that I missed a call from an unknown number. Whoever it was left a message; in fact, I had a couple of messages on my voicemail. How in the world did I miss so many calls? It must have been when I was buying all that Coach stuff. I guess I become deaf and dumb when I get in the stores.

The first message was from Charlene. She said since nobody else took the initiative, she would; Charlene made reservations for Evelyn, herself and I at some restaurant in Downtown Boston. She said if we had plans already for that date, we better cancel them. It was time for us to get back together and restore our friendship.

The next message was from Lance. He told me not to forget to do my crunches tonight. He said that my next husband, 'Ain't gonna want no fat belly chick'. He is a mess! The last call was from the unknown caller; it was Tim. He asked if I would call him back and that he'd like to get to know me better over some lunch. He said that he hoped I'd say yes and he'd wait for my call. I guess I'll have to take him up on that offer.

I'm headed to Marguerita's off of Route 28 for lunch with Tim. It's a nice day, about seventy degrees outside. The wind feels good as it brushes across my face. I get to the restaurant early; I'd rather be there waiting on him than to have him waiting on me.

I'm dressed casually; I have on a pair of fitted jeans, a white tank top, and a kelly green three-quarter sleeve sweater. I'm wearing my new Coach sneakers and matching belt. I look cute. My hair is pulled back in a sleek ponytail, exactly how Evelyn wears her hair.

I took my braids out and dyed my hair back to the light brown I've always worn. My lipstick is a peachy, copper color. It really makes my light eyes and light hair stand out. I have my Zoom black mascara by MAC on to give my eyes the flirty effect. I figured since I didn't put on anything sexy, I could at least look sexy from the neck up.

Not long after I get seated, Tim arrives. He's looking good and he's dressed casually too. He has on khaki cargo shorts, sandals, a white V-neck T-shirt and shades. He smiles as soon as he notices me. I greet him with a hug and he takes his seat.

"I thought for sure that I would beat you here."

"I guess you thought wrong," I say jokingly.

"Did you get a chance to order anything to drink yet?"

"No, I just had her give us water and I said she could come back once you got here."

"Okay, so how about I order for you once she gets here?"

"That's quite a risk you are taking. Things can go two ways. Either, you will order me something and I won't like it at all, which would really put a negative stamp on our first date. If you get it right, it may secure a second date with me."

"I think I will take that chance," Tim says confidently.

The lunch date went extremely well. Tim ordered five out of the seven entrees that they had. He figured I'd have to like one of them. I told him that he punked out by ordering so many dishes. He said that although he likes taking risks, he didn't want to risk losing the chance of taking me out again. That explanation is what got him a second date.

Tim and I started going out almost every night for dinner for two weeks straight. I told him that this had to be getting expensive, since he paid every time we went out. I also feared what the rich food was going to undo to my reclaimed physique. I'd been working out pretty hard, but because Tim was taking up a lot of my free time, I didn't get to the gym as much as I would have liked. We were going to have to slow things down and find other things to do.

The girls and I finally met up. It was awkward at first, but once we got a couple of drinks in us, we got to chatting, gossiping, and laughing throughout the whole night. We decided that we were going to meet up once a month at the same spot at the same time. We vowed that no matter how difficult life got, we would turn to each other, instead of away from each other. It felt good spending time with my crew.

Lance called. His voice sounded shaky as he told me about some homophobe he had an encounter with over the weekend. He said that some guy signed up for a trainer and asked to be signed up with the trainer that had the most clientele. He was assigned to Lance. Lance said the session was going fine, until a female client walked by and jokingly made a comment about the new client being his new boy toy. The new client got up from the bench and told the woman that he was nobody's boy toy. He then packed up his stuff to go. When Lance told him that he had another fifteen minutes, the guy said had he known Lance was a fag, he would have never signed up with him and he left. Lance acted as if he didn't care, but I knew that ordeal hurt him.

Evelyn:

I meet up with the girls to give them the bad news. At least I thought that it was bad news. I told them over dinner that I would no longer be able to meet for our monthly dinners. I was moving to California because Fritz got promoted. They were sad that they weren't going to witness my pregnancy progress, but wished me well and promised to fly out when the baby was born. I truly appreciated that.

In two weeks, I'd be moving to Cali. I told Fritz that I gave my notice at work, but I really just took a leave of absence. I needed a break from the non-profit world anyway. Being a program director was stressful. I was grateful that Fritz's new salary was going to be enough to support us without me working. It was really something I was going to have to get accustomed to.

I wondered what I was going to do all day. I was moving to a new place without a job to go to. Although we are married, I still like to have some type of financial autonomy. I wasn't really comfortable not having my own money to rely on. I would have to go to Fritz for everything and I was starting to have second thoughts about this move; it just didn't feel right. It felt like I was slipping on my mother's submissive shoes.

Two weeks went by quickly. Although I'm still in my first trimester, my girls Ava and Charlene managed to get my family and friends together and give me a baby shower. I was totally caught off guard. I received tons of gifts and gift cards to take with me. I was so overwhelmed about everything, I cried while I opened the gifts. I blamed it on the pregnancy.

When Fritz dropped me off at the shower, he said he'd pick me up when I was done. I begged him to come inside, but he said that baby showers were for women and that he was not coming in. I was disappointed, but I didn't fuss with him about it. He said he had a lot of stuff to do, because we were leaving tomorrow. He would be back when it was over. I had an attitude when I entered the hall, but it disappeared once I got in the company of my friends and family.

My husband never picked me up from the shower. I ended up being the last person to leave. I told everyone to go ahead and that Fritz would be here to get me soon. He was just running late. The truth was, I didn't know where this man was. I blew up his phone; I left so many messages that his phone could no longer take any voicemails.

Why would he not pick me up from the shower as he was supposed to? There was be no excuse. He better have been in a car accident or be somewhere stranded with no cell reception. He made me look so stupid; I was so embarrassed. Here we are, leaving to move across the country and he is so irresponsible that he forgets to pick me up from our baby shower. I mean, who does that? What the hell is wrong with him?

I end up taking a cab home, fussing all the way there. I get home and all of my stuff is packed in suitcases. When I left the house, all of my luggage was in the corner of the living room ready to be packed in the car. Since his job was paying for our housing in California, we decided to keep our place.

What he didn't know was that I was still paying the rent on the place I had before we moved in together. I never felt secure enough to let it go; I told myself that if something ever happened and I had to leave my home, I wasn't going to have to call a girlfriend to stay at her place. I definitely wouldn't have to call family. They get in your business too much.

It's now midnight. Fritz still has not called; I'm past being mad. Now I am worried sick. I've called police stations and hospitals and no luck locating Fritz. I felt like I was having an anxiety attack. I'd never had one so I wasn't sure. Up until this point, I hadn't made it into our bedroom.

I was so mad! I told myself that I wasn't going to let him sneak in; I was going to be sitting right on the couch waiting for him and his lies. Had I gone into the bedroom much earlier, I would have saved myself a lot of worrying. On my dresser, there was an envelope addressed to me. I rushed over to rip it open.

If I didn't read it with my own eyes, I wouldn't have believed it. This bastard left me and our baby. In the letter he wrote that since he got diagnosed with Fabry disease, life has been hard to deal with. A lot of the things that he wanted before, he no longer wants now. Things that were important to him before aren't important now. I guess that included me. He said that he wanted me to get an abortion, but didn't have the courage to ask me to. He talked about how stressed and depressed he's been. The bottom line was that he left to Cali without me.

Accompanying the letter were divorce papers. They were signed by him in advance. I couldn't breathe and I started to cry. My eyes became blurry with tears that felt like hot sauce. I fell to my knees and cried as if he died. From now on, that is how I will live my life; his funeral will be held tonight.

That's what I'll do; I will sign these divorce papers and pretend that he died. He might as well have. Fritz walked out on me. Not only me, but he also walked out on our unborn child. What am I supposed to tell everyone? I can't believe this is happening to me. I got enough sense to know that nothing is wrong with me. Something has to be wrong with him.

If he doesn't want me, I am not going to beg him to stay with me. He didn't even stick around long enough for me to beg anyway. As much as I would prefer to not be a single parent; I would rather raise my child alone than raise him in a house with a man that doesn't know how to love. It's amazing how a person can change almost overnight. Fritz was once the most selfless man I knew; and now he's the most selfish.

Charlene:

I never thought I could do pink dick, but Nate proved that pink was going to be my new favorite color! Once Nate did what my body needed him to do, I forgot all about his dick's color. It was time for our second girls' night out and I couldn't wait to tell them about who I was seeing. I know that I said that I was going to date all different types of men indiscriminately, but truth be told, Nate has been enough man to keep me seeking his time only.

He even openly flirts with me at work. I asked him to chill out. After all, I am the human resources director. I'm not exactly comfortable with my co-workers knowing my business, but so far, so good. There have been no awkward moments at work. Everyone at work loved my new makeover.

Nate wasn't the only white boy checking me out. I felt like I was the main character in a movie. Now, when I walk in rooms, ALL men stop and pay attention. Who knew I had this much sex appeal? I felt powerful!

I have a family reunion coming up soon. I mentioned it in front of Nate and he later asked me if he was invited. I told him that I didn't think he would be comfortable coming to that sort of engagement with me. He told me that I needed to ask myself if I would be comfortable with my new, white, boyfriend coming to the reunion. I smiled at him, because he called himself my boyfriend. I asked him who told him that he was my boyfriend; we've only been dating for a month. He said that nobody had to tell him that he was my boyfriend. He claimed the title and hopes to acquire more significant titles with me in the future.

I never confirmed that he was my boyfriend. If we are still going strong by the time my family reunion comes around, I will introduce him as my boyfriend, but I won't do it a second before then. It's only been a month; I'm sure he'll mess up before then. Something will happen. If he does make it to the reunion, then I am positive I will be the talk of the reunion. Next thing you know he'll be going to Kwanzaa celebrations with me.

As I get ready to go meet up with the girls, I feel my nose start to itch. It's itching right in the front hook part of my nostril. I'm home; nobody's around, so I decide to dig in my nose. What comes out is quite a specimen. I start to get paranoid and wonder how long it's been there. I think about all of the people I've come into contact with within the last hour. Because I picked my nose instead of going to the bathroom to get a tissue first and look in the mirror, I will never know if the boogie was hanging out a little.

I saw Nate before I left for the day. He didn't say anything. I hope he's not the type of person to let you have something on your face or in your teeth and not say anything. My girls and I talk shit about people that do that.

Ava:

Tim and I have been seeing a lot of each other. Things were going well. The last time we went out to dinner, I had ice cream for dessert. I think that I had too much ice cream. I dozed off on the ride home and woke up abruptly. I thought that maybe a beat in the music we were listening to woke me up. Then I realized he didn't have the music on!

I woke up to the "beat" of my ass; I'd farted! I was so embarrassed. He didn't say anything and I didn't know what to say. It was so awkward. My mother raised me to have manners, so I had to say excuse me. He looked at me and said, "Oh that's okay. I've been farting from the ice cream the entire time you were sleeping. I was secretly glad you were asleep." I looked at him and we both started cracking up simultaneously!

You forget about those things when you are in a relationship for a long time. When you are dating someone new, you have to get past the first fart, the first stinky bathroom episode, and so on. Dating someone new is great, because you get to reinvent yourself, but it could also leave you self-conscious. All of those lumps and dimples in those not-so-attractive places have to be rediscovered while you hold your breath and hope they don't mind. I think we, as women, mind more than the men do. I'm sure they aren't losing any sleep or stressing over any imperfections that they may have.

I'm going to blame it on television. They don't show any love scenes on TV where the woman has cellulite in her thighs. They don't show any women with saggy titties and stretch marks. When the women take off their clothes, you don't see any red marks across their stomach from their pants being too tight. Everyone on TV, magazines, and movies are perfect. So we strive to be perfect.

When diet and exercise alone don't work, some of us will go to a cosmetic surgeon to become as close to perfect as we can get. Tim and I have only kissed; I'm okay with that right now. Once we start sleeping together the game changes and feelings change. Things right now are safe and secure. There are no titles and no expectations attached to titles. He is still my "friend" Tim and not yet my "man" Tim.

Lance is coming over for dinner and a movie. To be exact, Lance is coming over for dinner and a series. He hipped me to *Noah's Arc*. He bought the box set on Amazon. We decided to watch at least two episodes a week and order in. I told myself that I was going to stop with all of this eating out and here I go committing myself to eating bad at least once a week until we finish the series.

I must say, the men in *Noah's Arc* are all good looking. Lance told me that not all of the actors are gay. I had a feeling that all of the main characters were. The one's that weren't gay were doing some good acting, because they had me fooled. Gay men and straight women seem to go through the same drama with the men we are involved with. Maybe that's why gay men and straight women get along so well. I wonder if gay men obsess over their body they way women do. I'll have to remember to ask Lance.

After Lance left, I called Tim to say good night. He asked what I was doing up so late. I told him that my friend just left and we just got finished watching a DVD. He asked what DVD we watched. I told him *Noah's Arc*. He laughed and said he couldn't believe that I was up so late watching Christian movies. I laughed and decided to let him believe I was watching the story about the real Noah and his ark.

Evelyn:

I figured that I might as well get it out of the way. I came clean with my family and friends and told them that Fritz and I were getting a divorce. Anyone that I didn't tell, I was sure that they'd find out from one of my family members or friends soon enough. My mom said that she was glad for me if that is what I wanted. I told her that I didn't know what I wanted, but I was sure I didn't want a man that didn't want me or my child.

Charlene and Ava were told on three-way. I let them ask all the questions that they wanted. Some I could answer and some I couldn't. They seemed to be just as shocked as, if not more than, I was. They were very empathetic. Ava and Charlene told me that they would be the daddy if Fritz didn't come to his senses and step up. I knew that they would be there for me.

After I got off of the phone with everyone, I went and got into my tub and took a hot bath laced with Palmer's Cocoa Butter Oil. I really needed to relax; I was stressed the hell out and I had a baby on the way, with no man. I needed a plan. I needed to think about my short-term and long-term goals.

I was now a single woman and single parent. Some things had to change and get rearranged. This child is going to have a good life despite the circumstances. After I got out the tub, I went to bed with a notepad to map out the next phase of my life. The next morning I head to the courthouse and submit the divorce papers. Fritz can kiss my black ass; it's his loss! Not only did I file for a divorce, but I tried to file for future child support.

I found out that I couldn't until the baby was born. He may try to abandon me, but he is not going to abandon his child. I'm glad he got that promotion, because he's going to support this baby. My child is going to reap the benefits of that promotion.

I'm not trying to be vindictive, but Fritz has to take some responsibility. I can't believe this coward said that he wanted to ask me to get an abortion. That's crazy, because I know he is voting for Romney. From what I've heard, Romney is pro-life. I should have known when he told me that he didn't vote for Obama in 2008 that things weren't going to work out for us. He just pushed and pushed for my hand in marriage.

In the end, I asked him to marry me. He definitely messed with my mind. He flipped it so that he had me asking for his hand in marriage. Then he asks me to walk away from this marriage. Everyone thought that I was the crazy one for not accepting his many proposals, and now they see what I feared all along. Once you get married, the demon comes out in people and things change.

I moved all of my things back to my place. As I'm looking out of the window, I notice a familiar form walking up my steps. I think that I am dreaming, because I haven't seen this man in years. He looks the same, just a little older. As soon as he comes up to my steps, I attempt to call 911. *How did he find me and why is he here?* He could only be here for one reason and that's to finish what he started all those years ago!

He smiles at me and says, "Every time I deliver mail and see the first name Evelyn, I secretly hope to run into you. I figured you would have a different last name by now. So who's the lucky man?"

I slam the door in his face. I couldn't help it. I was spooked. The last time this man was near me, he was trying to take my life. Now he was delivering my mail! I didn't have a restraining order against him. Even if I did, a lot of good that piece of paper would have done today. Those orders are good for future incidents. They aren't beneficial when the maniac shows up at your door.

As much of a headache as it was going to be to move my stuff back over to Fritz's, I was not going to stay here another night. He knows where I live. He knows my last name. I'd hoped that he'd be locked up by now for doing something crazy. You'd figure karma would have caught up with him; well karma's been slacking. She obviously hasn't caught up with him yet. He's still walking the streets. Who knows how many other girls have felt his wrath.

I left an hour after he left my place; I took everything I needed and decided that I would have a moving company move me. All of my things were in boxes anyway and my furniture could be put in storage. I was not going to live in fear, thinking he was going to come get me in the wee hours of the morning.

I get into my car and call Ava. Her phone went to voicemail. I then called Charlene. I haven't started my car yet. When she picks up, I start to tell her who I just saw and my plans to move back to Fritz's. As soon as I say John's name, I feel a sharp pain in my stomach and I drop the phone.

Next, I feel a sharp pain in my throat and see blood gushing out. As I'm losing consciousness, I hear him say, "That was supposed to be our baby you are carrying! You bitch! Who the fuck is Fritz! I told you our love would never die, but you will, bitch! You thought you could run away from me and that I wouldn't find you! Peek-a-boo bitch. I'm back!"

Ava:

Tim and I rush to the hospital as soon as I was told about Evelyn. Charlene and I were listed as emergency contacts. I called Charlene, but she was already on her way there. They got in touch with her first. I had my phone off because I was busy doing something I had no business doing so soon; I gave it up to Tim. There I was getting dick and I wasn't there when my friend needed me.

When I arrived, Charlene was already there. I could tell by the look on her face that things weren't good. Charlene said the phone went dead while they were talking. She figured Evelyn was in a bad area with limited reception. She called her right back and left her a message telling her to just call back when she gets in a good area. Right before the phone disconnected, she said John's name.

Charlene was praying that this had nothing to do with that psycho. I hope not either; I pray my girl is okay. I don't know what I'd do if she isn't okay. The doctor came out and asked for Charlene and I. He said that he couldn't help her; by the time she got to the ER, she had lost too much blood. He said that the man in the car with her was also unconscious and lost a lot of

121

blood, but they were able to save him. I couldn't believe my ears. Who the hell was in the car with her? Then it dawned on me. It was John!

John killed Evelyn! He must have tried to kill himself too, but he obviously didn't do it right. Dumb bastard! The doctor asked me if I knew John Stone, confirming everything that I thought. I told him that I did. He asked if I knew any family members and if I'd contact them. I told him that I did not. The only people that I would be trying to contact were the police. They saved a motherfucking murderer and let my girl die.

Evelyn was gone. Once I found out the details, all I could do was wail. This man stabbed her repeatedly in her stomach and slit her throat. She died a horrible death. He'd tried to kill himself and failed. He deserved to die. This felt like a horrible Lifetime Channel movie, except he was supposed to die too.

If I have anything to do with it, he will pay for taking away my best friend. Someone needed to tell Fritz. I decide to call and leave him a message, asking him to get back to me ASAP. That bastard never called me back. I couldn't take being at the hospital any longer and I asked Tim to take me home.

Tim offered to stay with me, but I really just wanted to be alone. My best friend died and I didn't want Tim to see me break down any more than he already has. I really couldn't process what happened. I tried to go to sleep, but I couldn't. I tried watching TV and I couldn't focus. When I did drift off to sleep, I kept dreaming about Evelyn being butchered with a knife. My screaming woke me up each time I drifted off. It was three am and I felt guilty for calling Charlene, but I needed to talk.

Charlene answered on the first ring. I asked if I woke her. She said she couldn't sleep either.

"It's really hard to believe that she's not here," Charlene whispered into the phone.

"I keep dreaming about her getting stabbed like in a horror movie."

"Evelyn used to say that John was going to come back to finish his handiwork."

"I know! I always thought she was being extra paranoid. She must have still been fearful."

"Ava, I don't know what to do with myself. I just want to go to the hospital and shoot John."

"I know how you feel, but we gotta let the law handle this one."

"I pray that he gets killed in jail. I want someone to take a mop handle and beat him to death."

"I hear ya. I know it's not Christian like to think or want those things, but he fucking deserves it."

"I can't imagine why God took her away from us. She was just getting ready to start a new life."

"She was starting a new life and going to produce one too. I miss her already Charlene."

After I got off the phone with Charlene, it was daylight. I decided to go to the gym. I called Lance and asked him if he was working today. He said that he would be at the gym by 7 am. I told him what happened and that I needed a good workout to ease some of the stress. He told me that he would pick me up, train me, and then take the rest of the day off to be with me.

Tim called me later while I was having lunch with Lance. Tim asked who I was with; I didn't really like his tone, but I overlooked it. I told him I was with Lance. He said that I told him that I wanted to be alone and yet now I was hanging out with Lance.

I really didn't have the energy to check him the way that I wanted to. I politely told him that I would call him when I got home later and that I was being rude to my friend being on the phone with him. He didn't wait for me to say goodbye. He disconnected the phone.

Lance and I had a great day. He really didn't try to distract me. He let me cry as many times as I needed to. He let me talk about Evelyn as often as I felt like it. By the time I got home, I felt better. That didn't last long. Two minutes after I closed my door, someone rang my buzzer.

It was Tim; I really wasn't in the mood to argue. When I let him in, he had this scowl on his face. I didn't bother to ask what his problem was; I honestly didn't care. I knew I would hear whatever his problem was soon enough. The first thing out of his mouth was how did I know that dude that dropped me off. I started to ask him how he knew that I got dropped off, but I didn't. I told him that the man, not dude, that dropped me off is my friend. Then he went on to say had he known that I hung around with faggots, he would have never got involved with me.

That comment really set me off. He was not going to come into my home and call my friend derogatory names. He knew what my last twenty-four hours had been like. Why was he being so damn rude? More importantly, how did he know Lance? When I asked him how he knew Lance, he said that he got trained by him once. He said that he had to change trainers when Lance hit on him.

Tim definitely wasn't Lance's type. I couldn't believe that Tim was the man that had Lance on the phone almost in tears. I can't believe I slept with this man. Had I just held out another night, he would have never gotten inside my panties. I asked Tim to leave. He huffed and puffed, talked a little shit and eventually left. I told him that I would pray for him. He gave me the finger as he exited and I yelled back, "That was so un-Christian like!"

Charlene:

Nate picked me up after Evelyn's funeral. I didn't have it in me to go to the dinner that was being prepared at her mom's house. I told Ava that I would talk to her tomorrow morning; I just needed to go home. Nate invited me to his house, but I just wanted to go home. He asked if I wanted some company; I didn't want to be rude, but Nate wasn't catching the hint. I just wanted to be alone.

I felt an attitude coming on. I quickly checked myself, because I knew that he was only trying to be supportive in my time of need. I gave him a big hug, a kiss, told him that I would be fine, and that if I needed him, I would call him. He left reluctantly. I watched him out the window until he got into his car and drove off.

As I was watching Nate, I think to myself; *what am I going to do with this white man?* Could I really see myself with him long-term? Would color ever become an issue? What about kids? I really needed to evaluate my life and my life plans. I could tell that Nate was trying to get serious. I've just been dodging the conversation.

I didn't know what to do. I had too much going on. Evelyn is gone and a white guy wants to be my man. I wished Evelyn was here. She always had logical helpful advice. I actually dialed her number a few days ago to tell her something funny. Then I remembered that she was gone. She died such a horrible death. What's really messed up is that her father didn't even show up to her funeral. Her mom said that he wasn't feeling well. I knew the deal. He and Evelyn had a volatile relationship.

I really believe that they hated each other. I don't care what type of relationship I have with my kid. God forbid that they die before me you best believe I will be at their funeral. He's going to go to hell for that. Every time I think about it, my eyes fill up. I want to cry for Evelyn. She's had such awful relationships with the men in her life. I get a lump in my throat.

Usually, when I have a lot going on, I listen to Mary to clear my head. Today, I'm listening to Lil Wayne. Nobody would ever guess that he would be one of my favorite rappers. Every now and then I find myself quoting his lyrics. He's very creative and clever. Don't get me wrong, some of the language he uses is offensive, but I still listen to him. Shit, some of the language I use is offensive too.

125

After I finish listening to Lil Wayne, I decide to go to the mall. Going to the mall always makes me feel good. I don't even have to buy anything to feel good. I get a second wind whenever I enter the mall. I look in a few stores that I have no business being in. The prices are out of my budget. I still buy a few things that I don't need. I then walk to the music store and buy all the music that I've been meaning to buy.

As I'm leaving Newbury Comics, I see a familiar face working at the Verizon Wireless booth. I was going to act as if I didn't see him, but then we made eye contact, so I had to speak. As soon as I get to the booth, he's trying to sweet talk me. Don't get me wrong, this man has charm and is still looks as sexy as ever.

I just couldn't get past the fact that he was working in a mall, at a Verizon booth, trying to sell cell phone and plans. He asked me was I seeing anyone. I told him that I was, but that's all the info that I would give. I wouldn't dare tell him that he was white. He'd have a field day with that info. I kept our conversation short and lied about having somewhere to be. I wonder if Derek will ever change. The fact that I could walk away without a tear or a feeling of sadness proved that he was finally out of my system.

I called Nate as I was driving home. I asked him to come over so that we could talk about our relationship. He said that he would be over in an hour. That gave me just enough time to shower and change into something cuter than what I was wearing. Tonight, I was going to tell Nate that he and I could be a couple. I wanted to make sure that we were both up for whatever that may entail.

Nate acted as if he was the luckiest man in the world when I told him I was ready to become a couple. He couldn't keep his hands off of me. He couldn't keep his mouth off me either. There wasn't a body part or crevice that he didn't orally explore. Not even "Weekend Charlene" ever had anyone do her like that.

I must admit, it felt good, but it made me not want to kiss him after. When he went home for the night, I started feeling differently about him. I was kind of grossed out and I started wondering if this is how good he made all of his girlfriends' feel. Is there such a thing as being too intimate with your boyfriend?

The next morning I got my answer. Last Friday, I went for my annual pap smear. I got a call from my gynecologist on Monday that my test came back positive for Chlamydia! I was totally embarrassed and then the anger came. My doctor told me that she'd be calling in a prescription for me to pick up at CVS.

Besides Nate, I haven't been with anyone since Derek. So that means Nate is the culprit. I knew that my feelings of ambivalence were warranted. This nasty motherfucker has been sleeping around. What he did to me last night was something he's probably done many times before.

I'm grateful I got something that could be cured with a pill, but this jackass could have killed me. I thought that we were in a monogamous relationship. We stopped using condoms less than two weeks ago. Lesson learned.

I thought about doing something really vindictive; I thought about how things could have been worse. The call could have come from my GYN stating that I am HIV positive. So instead, I silently thanked God. Then I left Nate a nasty voicemail telling him to get himself treated and make sure whatever other woman's asshole he's eating out gets treated too. I then called in sick to get my head together. No more white men for me.

I thought about calling Evelyn, but then I remembered that she's in heaven. I called Ava and told her what happened. She said that she's gotten that call too. She said she got that call while she was married. It was gonorrhea; imagine how that feels getting it from your husband. I couldn't imagine. I guess there's no safety in relationships or even something as sacred as marriage. I wonder if I will ever find a good man.

I still have hope that there's a man out there that will love me, provide for me and be loyal to me. I want a man that is willing to work four jobs if necessary, just so I don't have to work one. I want a man that will have dinner waiting for me when I come home. I'm looking for a man that will surprise me with vacations where I don't have to pay half the cost for it like Ava's no good ex-husband Brian. In Derek's case, I would have had to pay for all of it.

I just want a good, God-fearing man that will make me forget all of the other men of my past. Ava told me that I needed to be careful and not become bitter like she did. I told her that it's too late. I am already bitter; I've gone through too much with these men to not become bitter. Unfortunately, the next man is going to have to pay for some of the crimes my ex's committed. He will have to work extra hard to earn my trust and win me over.

It's sad that I've become bitter. It's even sadder that men have mishandled me to the point where I'd become this way. It's their fault that I'm this way. Ava and I decided to have a girlfriend's weekend twice a year. It will be a time to dedicate to taking care of our mind body and soul. Evelyn always advocated for taking time out for oneself and hitting up a spa. We've decided to try out a new spa, each year, in a new location. Evelyn would be proud of us. Who knows, maybe we will meet our future husbands on one of our spa trips. Until then, we will be Duracell sisters!

Ava:

After dating Tim, I've dated a few other guys here and there. Nobody has made me want to be in a committed relationship with them. I'm starting to worry that Mr. Right will never find me. I'm at the age where I need to decide if I want to have children or not. Time's running out.

You figure if you meet someone it will take you at least a year to decide if you want to marry them. Once that decision is made, then it takes another year or so to get married. After that, you can start to plan for a child. That's already 2 years of foundation needed before I would even begin to start trying for a child. That's so much pressure and so little time!

Lance told me that he'd make a child with me if I ever needed him to. Now that's a good friend. Let's hope I don't have to take him up on that offer. I asked him if he ever had sex with a woman. He said that he did while he was in high school. It wasn't until college that he had his first encounter with a man. He said that he'd shut his eyes and imagine it was Wade from Noah's Arc if he ever had to impregnate me. I laughed and told him that I would imagine I was with Idris Elba.

I lost one friend and gained another. God sure works in mysterious ways. I got some surprising news last week; Fritz passed away. He never got treatment while he was in California. His kidney ended up failing. I told Charlene about Fritz. She said that she was sorry to hear it, but I don't think she was. She still held a grudge against him for leaving Evelyn and on top of that, not showing up for her funeral.

I told Charlene that she needed to start forgiving the people that have hurt her. It hurts her way more than it will hurt them. When you become bitter, you do all types of crazy things. I told her that I almost lost my mind dealing with Brian. I don't want her to end up how I was. I did some things that I never imagined myself doing, because I was hurt. I'm still hurt, but I can honestly say that I am no longer bitter.

Even after dealing with finding out that Brian had twins with his whore, I'm not bitter. Even after hearing that he got some job through a friend of friend making six figures, I'm not bitter. This man got a new car, a new family, a new job and life for him appears to be better than what it was when we were together. Good for him. I'm still not bitter.

You know why? I'm not bitter because I've moved on and prayed about it. When I was done praying, I started doing his fine ass brother Ben. Let's see how Brian feels about that. Trust, I am going to make sure that he finds out about it. Checkmate!

BITTER ENDINGS

Ben:

    I know that my brother would disown me if he knew that I was sleeping with his ex-wife, but I just can't get enough of Ava. When Brian first introduced her to me as his girlfriend, I felt that she should have been my lady. She wasn't even his type. I have no idea why he married her. I sometimes think that he did it just to make me jealous. He knew that I was attracted to her. I told him that same night that he introduced her to me.

    I teased him by asking what he was doing with a woman like Ava. He couldn't possibly know what to do with her. Guess what? I was right! He didn't know how to keep her. If he knew how to keep her, she wouldn't be coming over every other night, begging me to dick her down. I mean things get real nasty with us; I have no idea how my brother could leave a piece of ass like this.

    Yes, I call her a piece of ass, because that is all she will ever be to me, but I'd never say it to her face. She can't possibly think that we could have something serious, after she's been married to my brother. Now, I may be scandalous enough to go behind my brother's back and sleep with the same woman that he was married to, but I would never get into a committed relationship with the woman!

At some point, Ava and I are going to have to stop sleeping with each other. I will admit that I'm not looking forward to giving up this fine specimen. She is addictive; she does it all. Ava gives head and swallows! I haven't met a black woman willing to swallow since college! And even that one wasn't a sister-sister. She was half and half.

I figured her white ancestry is what made her agreeable to get down like that. So you see, Ava is not going to be someone that I can let go of easily now that I've had a taste. The first time that we had sex, I made her promise not to tell anyone, especially anyone that's linked to Brian. I told her as much as I loved what just went down with us, I couldn't risk hurting my brother. I told her that he would be devastated, because Brian's like my best friend. She said that she understood and would keep our arrangement to herself. She better.

Ava's not my only lady. She didn't ask and I didn't tell her. I'm also doing her friend Charlene; I know that sounds grimy, but I am actually really feeling Charlene. She looks like Zoe Saldana. She has that exotic flavor to her. People often mistake her for Zoe when we are out. I guess she looks like Zoe with a good tan.

One night, while we were out to dinner, an older white guy came over and complimented her. He told her that he loved her in the movie *Columbiana*. She got a kick out of that. She thanked him and he went on about his way. I can see myself marrying Charlene one day; she's perfect for me.

She is funny, smart, sexy and giving. She always shows appreciation. I guess that has a lot to do with some guy named Derek she was engaged to. She said that she had to foot the bill all the time when they were together. Derek sounds like he went to the same school as my cheap-ass brother. The most Brian would do is go half on a bill, and I've told him that he would never be able to get a woman with that type of mentality. I guess he proved me wrong. He got Ava, but look at who has her now. Charlene told me that she had a falling out with Ava. Having that information gives me a sense of security.

If Charlene doesn't talk to Ava anymore, then there is no way that either of them will find out that I'm sleeping with both of them. God has truly blessed me. Now if he would only turn Charlene into a swallower!

Ava:

Charlene and I were supposed to have our spa weekend and she bailed out on me. We have had this planned for months. I paid up front for the both of us. Since she has cancelled on me, I have to either waste her portion of the package or find someone else at the last minute. I really didn't want to go with anyone else. I decided to give my mom and my aunt the package. You know that I was desperate if I gave it to my mom.

Thank God that the location was a couple of hours drive away or else I would have wasted plane tickets too. When I found out that Charlene was backing out of the trip, I went off on her. I was so disappointed; I needed this trip. The last two years have been chaotic. I needed a haven to escape to so that I could de-stress. Charlene really wouldn't give me a good explanation as to why she wasn't going; she just said that she wasn't feeling up to it.

Well, that type of an explanation was not good enough for me. The old Ava resurfaced and I continued to cuss her out. By the end of the call, I told her to swallow a razor blade; she disconnected the call after I made that remark.

Since Evelyn's death, Charlene has been the only one that I share my dirt with besides Lance. Lance is great, but Charlene and I go way back. So, although Ben asked me to keep it a secret, I told Lance about Ben and I. Lance told me to be careful. He said that I could be putting myself in harm's way messing with Brian's brother. I told him that the dick is worth it.

133

He was silent for a second. Then he laughed and said that he understood all too well about risk-worthy dick!

I missed my trip to the spa and on top of that, Ben says he'll be busy this weekend and has no time to hang out with me. I don't know what he is talking about. We don't ever hang out; all of our business is done in the privacy of his home. Speaking of his home, his house reminds me of the homes on HGTV that have gotten a makeover. It looks like he had a designer come in and hand pick everything.

His master bathroom is the size of my bedroom. It has a fireplace with white marble. The floor is heated. He has copper double sinks with a penny-colored granite. His tub is one of those old-fashioned claw foot tubs that you just want to soak in. The shower has lights and multiple jets. It is big enough for three people to fit comfortably. His toilet has a remote control and closes on its own. And there's a flat screen TV and chaise lounge inside the bathroom. Brian told me that his brother made money; with the design and décor of the bathroom, I am getting a feel for just how much money Ben must make.

It's too bad that I didn't marry Ben, instead of Brian's cheap behind. My life would have been so much better. This bathroom would be my bathroom. Shit, this house would be my house. I would be driving the 760-Series BMW that I deserve. Life would be better than good, life would be great!

I have absolutely nothing planned this weekend. Lance knew that I was going away so he made plans with one of his friends. Charlene and I weren't speaking. Ben was going to be too busy for me this weekend. I guess I needed to spend some quality time with myself. I decided to go to one of my many toy catalogs and get some toys overnighted. I also bought some videos to get some pointers on how to turn Ben out! I guess I would spend this weekend pleasing myself after all.

When my package arrived, I couldn't wait to get started. I'd purchased a new dildo, a vibrator that has a life-size tongue attached to it and two adult films. One of the films Lance recommended. It was guy on guy, but he said I could learn a thing or two from it. The other film was girl on girl. Since I wasn't down with a threesome, I figured that the next time Ben and I had sex, I could play this while we did it.

This would give him the illusion of having more than one woman. I watched the guy on guy film and I really didn't see anything that I could learn from it. Although, I must admit, some of those guys could give me a run for my money in the head department. I thought I had skills; these men could suck the skin off of a dick.

Then I moved on to the girl on girl action. I don't know if I was turned on by the sound of them moaning or just because I hadn't gotten any from Ben in a few days. But that film had me with the vibrator on full speed, feeling like I was ready to pee my pants! I will definitely be bringing this film to Ben's house next week.

That was my Saturday. On Sunday, I took myself out to brunch. Then I rented some regular movies and stayed in for the rest of the day; I had a good weekend with no stress and no drama.

Evelyn's murderous ex-fiancé got life in prison, only because Massachusetts doesn't have the death penalty. I know that I should let things be and let him suffer in jail, but for some reason that was not good enough for me. I wanted his stay to be as uncomfortable as possible; I wanted it to be torturous. I left a message for Craig. I needed him to arrange something for me.

Charlene:

Life has been great. I have a new man that treats me so much better than Derek ever did. Nate treated me well until that STD. I've been dating Ben, Brian's brother, for about six months now. I didn't know how to tell Ava, so I kept it to myself. Ben had an important work-related banquet to attend and begged me to go with him. I told him that I would go. I didn't realize it was the same weekend as our spa weekend until I already committed myself to going.

When I told Ava that I couldn't go, I knew that she was going to flip her wig. I wanted to tell her the truth, but I couldn't because I had yet to tell her that I was seeing Ben. It just never seemed to be the right time to tell her. At first, I said to myself that I would tell Ava after my first date with him. Then I changed my mind and said I will tell her if I sleep with him. After that, I told myself that I would tell her after I figured out if this could be something serious. Well, now we are at the point of seriousness. Ben proposed to me and I accepted at his company's banquet.

There was going to be no way that I could hide an engagement ring from Ava, but I don't have to worry about that now. After the way she cussed me out, I don't know if I will ever be close to her again. That bitch told me to swallow a razor. Well, she can choke on my big, five-carat engagement ring!

Ben asked me what date we should set the wedding date for; I told him that he could decide. He said not only would he decide, but he would do the planning for me too. I laughed and told him that he had no experience with planning a wedding. He told me that he had money to pay a wedding planner to take care of everything. All that I had to do was show up.

Ben was my dream man. So far, there wasn't anything about him that I didn't like. Don't get me wrong. He was not perfect, but he was turning out to be perfect for me. Everything that he couldn't do, he had the means to be able to pay someone to do it. That is my type of man! He treats me like a queen. I will say that he is a little freakier than expected in the bedroom, but I am not complaining.

Ben gave me a $10,000 wedding gown budget. That is way more than I would ever spend on a gown. I still have my last gown hanging in the closet; I need to do something with it.

Maybe I could donate it to charity; it's never been worn. Maybe I could sell it on eBay; no doubt, somebody will buy it.

I start looking through bridal magazines and I feel lonely. The last time I was looking for dresses Evelyn and Ava helped me. Now I have neither of them helping me. Life sure knows how to throw curveballs at you. I'm finally happy. I'm marrying a good man and I don't have my girls to celebrate with. One is dead and the other might as well be. I need to make some new friends anyway.

Ava:

Craig finally called me back. He didn't trust phones, so he told me to meet him at his spot. When I got there, it seemed as though a party was going on. People were playing Spades. Some were dancing to the music, while others were in the back smoking weed. I didn't see Craig anywhere. When I came back outside, I saw him getting out of his car. This fool told me to come over and he wasn't even home yet.

I walked back into his place and we went into his room to talk. He told me that he had some fellas on the inside that would take care of what I needed. I was so grateful that I hit him up with five thousand dollars for arranging this for me and told him that I owed him. The plan that I came up with for John was evil; it was for some inmate to make him their bitch; I wanted him raped repeatedly.

At first, I just wanted someone to kill him, but then I later learned that not only did this sick creep kill Evelyn, but he had sex with her once she was dead. The bastard had the nerve to fail at killing himself. It was then that I decided that I wanted him to be raped until he wished he was dead.

Not only did I want him raped, but I wanted the person raping him to have the virus so that it passed on to John. I wanted him to suffer. I know that this is sick of me to even think of, but it is what it is. I also arranged for the same man that is going to do the raping to save his shit daily and have some inmates force-feed it to him every night. I figure a daily raping, force-fed shit and contracting HIV, will make him want to get it right this time and kill himself.

If he lasts an entire year, I'd be surprised. I would revisit the idea of having him killed if he made it. Now that I've taken care of that order of business, I need to figure out just how I'm going to reveal to Brian that I'm sleeping with Ben. Just telling him wouldn't be enough. I'm leaning towards videotaping us during one of our nasty sessions and then posting it on his FB for everyone to see. Brian will pay for doing me wrong. He'll keep paying until I don't hurt anymore.

He forgets that I still have his account info and can log on anytime to post my sex tape. My next stop is to the tech store that has all of those surveillance gadgets, disguised as everyday objects. Ben definitely wouldn't be onboard with me putting a camera in front of us while we do it. So, I'm going to have to resort to these measures to accomplish my goal. This store has all types of gadgets. It was inspiring me to take up private investigating as a side gig. I ended up purchasing sunglasses, a pen and a decorative ornament. They all had tiny cameras inside. The range in which they could cover was amazing. They cost me a pretty penny, but it will all be worth it.

I called Ben and made a date for tomorrow night. I told him that I bought some toys for us to explore. He was excited and so was I. After tomorrow night, I am going to have to kick Ben to the curb. As much as I enjoy his company, he's going to hate me almost as much as his brother will when I leak this video.

There was no need for me to beat around the bush. I showed up at Ben's house in a thin coat, with nothing on underneath. We both knew what I came for. He just didn't know that what I came for would be filmed tonight. I decided to use the glasses and the pen as surveillance devices.

When I came in, I placed my Coach pocketbook on his dresser. I then acted like I was looking for something in my bag. I pulled out my sunglasses and my pen. When I had them strategically placed, I miraculously found the lip gloss that I wasn't really looking for.

As I was putting on my lip gloss, he came behind me and unbuttoned my coat. From that point, it was on. I played the girl on girl video for him to get things started. I spread myself out on the bed and let him watch me please myself with my new toys. Watching me and having the video playing in the background really had him going. He wanted me so badly; he was drooling.

After my kinky performance, I was ready for the real shit to take place. We did all types of freaky things. The only thing that I didn't do was swallow. I only did that before to keep him coming back for more. Since this would be our last night, I really didn't need to go the extra mile pleasing him.

I knew he would be pleased regardless, because I have skills in the bedroom. I could give seminars to the meek inexperienced females out there. There is definitely an art to having sex and I've mastered it. When we were done, I had all of the footage that I needed. He actually helped me out more than he will ever know. Not only was he really into it, but he was full of himself.

He started yelling that he bet Brian never put it down the way he did. I just played along and agreed that Brian never made me feel this good. Once I started complimenting his dick, it was over. He came quickly, and that was the end of it. After I took my shower, I went home to edit my new film.

I must say it was a good film. If I was into the adult film industry, this would be a great resume for me. I called in sick the next day, because I was up all night editing. This had to be perfect; I wanted Brian to see every thrust his brother delivered. The good news was that I didn't have to fake it his brother did know how to put it down. He was a lot better than Brian.

Ben:

Damn, Ava put it on me last night. Charlene wanted to come over and talk about wedding stuff, but I wasn't going to pass up a night with Ava. I could see Charlene another time. We are about to get married and be with each other forever. I needed to get as much of Ava as I could. Believe me, if there was a way to keep Ava and still marry Charlene, I would. I know this is going to end once I get married, but I'm going to ride this out until the very last hour.

Charlene's here now, and we are going over the plans with the wedding planner. We could potentially get married within about three months if she wants to do it that soon. I'm hoping that she wants to drag it out a little longer, so that I can get some of what Ava's got for a little while longer. She is so good that she should be getting paid for her services.

Charlene decided that she wants to have the wedding on Valentine's Day. That was four months away. That would be enough time to get Ava out of my system. After Charlene leaves, I call Ava and ask her if she wants to come over and hang out. She usually jumps at the chance. Tonight she said that she was tired and wasn't feeling up to it, she just wanted to stay in. I offered to come over to her house and she still rejected me. With Charlene at home and Ava not wanting to come out and play, I was left with one option. I had to handle my business alone. Ava let me have that girl on girl video. It worked like a charm.

Ava has been dodging me for one reason or another for a month now; something has changed. She is not feeling me anymore and I can't figure out why. The last time we had sex, it was great. I don't remember saying anything to make her mad. Why is she all of a sudden playing hard to get?

I must say with Ava not around, it has given me time to really get involved with this wedding planning. I've paid for everything and now all we have to do is just wait for February 14th to get here. Our colors will be red, black and white. All of the floral arrangements will be red and white roses. Our cake will be made into a big red heart, with a plastic miniature version of the bride and groom sitting on top.

While we were going over the list of guests to mail invitations to, I noticed that she had Ava down as a guest. I asked Charlene if she was sure that this is the way that she wanted Ava to find out about our relationship. She thought about it, took the invite out of the pile, and placed it in her purse. I needed February 14th to get here ASAP. If Ava found out I was doing both her and her former best friend, there may not be a wedding.

Ava:

Craig just gave me a progress report. From what he tells me, John is on suicide watch. I tell Craig to keep me posted as he gives me a head nod. All of a sudden, I'm now in a good mood. It must be from the good news I got from my cousin Craig.

Last Saturday was Valentine's Day. I had a date, but then I cancelled it. I wasn't in the mood to hang out and drink; I just wanted to stay home and relax. It's not as if I had anybody that I considered special in my life. It took about two months of nonstop calling, but Ben finally got the hint. I never called him again and he never called me.

Today is February 21st. It is Brian's birthday and he has lots of postings on his page about a birthday party at his house. He sent out at least thirty invites. I sent all of those invites a message from Brian's page. The message said look at what my brother got me for my birthday.

When the reader opens it, they see Ben and I going at it. Once I sent the messages, I immediately felt at peace. By tonight, Brian will feel the hurt that I've felt since he did me wrong. There's nothing like witnessing your husband having sex with another woman. There's also nothing like seeing your ex-wife letting your brother devour her.

I was walking around the house singing. I was feeling so good, I decided to go shopping. I went out and bought myself a brand-new pair of knee-high leather boots. I also bought myself a new pea coat. When I got home; I was beat so I made some tea, took a bath, and then went straight to bed. The next morning when I woke up, I got the urge to go to church.

Not only did I go to church, but also I walked up that aisle to be saved and baptized. Now that I've gotten that bitter-ass monkey off my back, life could begin again. When I got home, something didn't feel right. I couldn't put my finger on it, but something was off. I put down my Bible and decided to go to my room. I looked in my top drawer to see if any of my jewelry was missing; nothing was gone. All of my electronics were accounted for. I checked every room in my place, trying to make sure that nobody was in this house with me uninvited. I even checked the closets.

I made some tea and started running some bath water. After drinking the tea, I felt extremely sleepy. I decided to take a nap and nix the bath. When I woke up, I was naked and my coochie hurt as if someone jabbed a hair brush up there; I was also tied up. That's when I knew that this wasn't going to be a good night; hell, I'd be lucky if I made it through the night.

Ben was at my house; drunk, high, or both. I don't know. What I do know is that he was talking a bunch of crazy shit. He told me that since I broke my promise not to tell anyone about our arrangement, he felt that he could break in my house and have his way with me in my sleep. As he was talking, I wondered why my face and head felt wet. My hands were tied up, so I couldn't touch my head. I hoped I wasn't bleeding.

I wasn't bleeding. This whack job came on my face and forehead multiple times! He raped me. He told me that if I even thought about going to the police with this, that he wouldn't kill me, but would have someone else do it. Ben had a lot of money and a lot of people around him willing to do things for money. I knew he was serious.

After he slapped me a couple of times for not returning his calls, he forced himself inside me yet again, for the third, fourth or tenth time. Who knows how many times he raped me. Before he left, he untied my arms, but left my feet tied. I guess that was to give him enough time to leave. It wouldn't have mattered if he untied my hands and feet. I could hardly move. What I couldn't figure out was why is it that I didn't wake up when he was raping me.

He had to have drugged me. The way that my coochie was feeling, there was no way I could have slept through that. I went to work the next day as if nothing happened to me. I went to work every day that week. I think that I was still in shock. I was not performing as I should and I knew it. I decided to put in for some vacation time. I had a month that I could take off. I put in for two weeks. If I needed another two after that, I would take it.

I tried to nurse my coochie back to health during my time off. I didn't sleep with anyone. I didn't douche. And when my period comes, I wasn't using any tampons. The problem was that my period didn't come. Ben was the only person I've been with, but we always used protection. I don't know what that psycho did to me a few weeks ago, but I wouldn't put it past him to have not used protection.

My gut tells me that if I'm late, I must be pregnant. And I was right. The bastard didn't have the decency to use a condom and raped me raw. I was now pregnant with my rapist ex-brother- in-law's child. Could God be any crueler? Was I going to keep this baby or abort it? I really considered aborting it, but then I thought that there may be some way to get back at Ben through this child.

I haven't figured it out yet, but I would make sure that I'd lay low until this baby is born. I wouldn't want Ben to find out and then he'd have someone try to kill me. The more I thought about it, the more having this baby would be a blessing. I might get that 760-Series BMW after all; Ben will have to pay child support once the baby gets here. I will have the court order a paternity test. Once it is proven that he is the father, my child support payments will be substantial! I might be able to become a stay-at-home mom. This pharmaceutical job was getting old quick. All I needed to do is get through this pregnancy.

Finally, I'm far enough along in my pregnancy to have found out the sex. I am having, excuse me, Ben and I are having a girl. Brian never contacted me about sleeping with his brother. That's okay though. I know that he saw the video. Ben wouldn't have come over and raped me if his brother had not seen the video. I'd sent it to all of his friends and family, so I know he was devastated, which is exactly what I wanted.

I kind of feel bad that I had to use his brother to get back at him, but that bitch karma came around, and made things even between Ben and I. Karma played such a big role in my life, I decided to name our child Karma.

Charlene:

Ben and I are now married and life is good. I moved into his house and sold mine. I kept the money from the sale of my home and invested it; I always wanted to invest. I told myself when I did invest, it wouldn't be with chump change. Now I am in a position to do it. Ben told me that I could quit my job if I wanted. I'd have nothing to do if I quit my job so, I told him that I wanted to continue to work.

I'm starting to think differently about that decision. I found out recently that I am pregnant. My periods have always been kind of off, so I really didn't pay any attention to my missed periods. When I had my annual GYN exam, the doctor told me that I was pregnant. I wasn't sure how Ben was going to react.

I know that he wants kids, but we talked about having them further down the line. We wanted to enjoy our marriage first, but I guess God had different plans. Now our first year of marriage will include preparing for our first child. Thinking back, I was really sick the night of Brian's birthday party. I had to stay home and let Ben go alone. That was probably an indication of my pregnancy.

The baby is supposed to be born on October 4. We are both so excited. It's already September and our baby will be here before you know it! I'm having a girl. We've decided to name her Evelyn Ava Ford. Ben wasn't too happy about making her middle name Ava. He was dumbfounded by my decision since Ava and I haven't spoken in such a long time, but I was adamant. Evelyn and Ava were like sisters to me.

I pray at some point Ava and I can rekindle our friendship. I've forgiven her for lashing out at me. Too much has happened since then that she wasn't a part of. I'm not sure if she would even want to reunite. Well if it is meant to be, it will be. Until then, I have a baby to worry about.

Ben:

Ever since Brian's party, things have not been the same. We had a big falling out. I was heated; I'm not sure how my episodes with Ava got filmed, but I wouldn't put it past her to have facilitated it. I was so drunk that night. I ended up stalking Ava; I waited until she went out the next morning and hid under her bed.

I knew her routine, so it was easy for me to slip her a date rape pill. I put it in her tea that she has before she settles down for bed. Except I didn't have to wait until bedtime; she made some tea when she came in from church. I waited for it to take affect and then I had the roughest sex I was capable of performing with her. Nothing was off limits. And you best believe she swallowed this time!

After I left, I felt a twinge of guilt, but that went away quickly. That bitch knew that she was wrong for making a sex tape without my knowledge and then leaking it. I know she wasn't trying to hurt me, but she did. Luckily, Charlene was sick that night and didn't come to the party, or else she would have found out too. Charlene would have been another casualty of Ava's messy war.

I threatened Ava with death if she tried to go to the cops about me raping her. She knows that I don't play around. Even if she did report it, it wouldn't get far. I have my connections at the precinct. I just don't need that type of a headache. I was going to tell her to stay away from Charlene too. After I thought about it, I didn't need to tell her that. She still had no idea that Charlene and I were involved.

Ava:

I'm due at the end of September. That time is creeping up. I've been laying low throughout my pregnancy. In the beginning, I was not really excited about carrying this baby. Since I've been going to church regularly and got baptized, I've come to really appreciate this pregnancy. It doesn't matter how it happened. There is a mini-me growing inside of me.

Now don't get me wrong; I am still going to file for child support from Ben. I heard that he got married. I bet his wife won't appreciate the fact that he has another child. Oh well! I'm not concerned about that girl's feelings. I just want to make sure that Karma gets what she deserves; her daddy's money.

It's too bad Charlene and I stopped speaking. I would have made her Karma's godmother. She would have been a great godmother for Karma. I really miss her. I know that I shouldn't have gone off on her the way that I did. Telling her to swallow a razor blade might have been a little too far. I was just so upset and disappointed.

I've forgiven her. I wonder if she has forgiven me. Maybe I will reach out to her and apologize after the baby is born. Even if she doesn't want to fix our friendship, I still owe her an apology. I've just had so much going on in my life. I need all of the friends I can get.

Lance has been a great help. He gave me a baby shower at his house. Lance is the only one that knows who the baby's father is. I was too ashamed to tell my mom, so I said it was from a one-night stand. Nevertheless, she can't wait for Karma to get here. I don't know why, when she treated me like shit. Why would she be excited about her daughter's child?

Since it is getting close to my due date, I've been given permission to work from home. Thank God, because it was getting harder and harder to get up and come into work. I needed the money, so I went. I am going to be a single parent living on one income, at least until Ben's child support kicks in. Lance told me that he would be Karma's father figure and then transition into her uncle figure when I got a new man. Lance is just the sweetest.

Needless to say, after I got my figure back, I lost it again once I got pregnant. Lance told me that he would have me back to my regular size within six months. I can't wait. It's hard being pregnant and fat. It's hard going up stairs. It's hard sleeping at night. My feet hurt. My hips hurt. I am just so uncomfortable. My obstetrician scheduled me for a C-section on October 4. I guess I'll be having this baby sooner than expected.

Charlene:

Today is the most wonderful day of my life. Evelyn Ava Ford was born at 10:04 am, today, October 4th. She is so beautiful! She looks just like Ben. God has been so good to me. After Evelyn died, I didn't think life would ever be joyful, but God heals your heart and makes it so that you are able to laugh and love again. I have a new husband and a new baby. I have a new life!

I can go home the day after tomorrow. I can't wait to bring Evelyn home. I just couldn't see putting her in her nursery, so I had Ben pull the crib in our bedroom so that I could be near her. She is so precious. I never knew I could love someone this much.

Ben's been acting edgy lately. He usually leaves his work problems at the door. That hasn't been the case recently. He seems to have no time for the baby and I. He's been meeting with his lawyer about financial stuff more so than he usually does. I wonder what's going on; I know if I ask him, he'll tell me that everything is fine and not to worry, but I know something is up.

Ava:

They pulled this baby out of me at 8 am on the dot, October 4. Karma is the most beautiful baby that I have ever seen. She looks just like Ben. She even has his good hair. She has my light brown eyes and my lips. She is going to look better than Beyoncé, Halle and myself combined!

I had the court order a paternity test for Ben. The drama that I avoided during my pregnancy months will reconvene soon enough. I never told him that I was pregnant. I never saw him or spoke to his crazy ass after that night. Like I said, the only person that knew was Lance. Even Lance didn't know that he raped me. He just thought we had an accident.

Lance called me and said that he ran into Charlene at the South Shore Plaza Mall coming out of a children's store yesterday. He said that she had a baby. Lance told me she named her Evelyn Ava Ford. When Lance said Evelyn Ava, I totally blocked out the last name. It wasn't until I got over the shock of her middle name that I realized what her last name was. I'm assuming that Charlene got married. She married someone with the last name of Ford. That was weird. We both married a man with the last name of Ford. I wonder if they were some type of relation to each other.

Well Lance held the kicker until the end. Charlene definitely married someone related to Brian Ford; she married Ben Ford. God sure has a sense of humor. Lance went on to tell me that she had the baby on the same day I had Karma. That means he was fucking Charlene at the same time he was fucking me.

I asked Lance if she asked about me. He said that she didn't. I asked him if he mentioned anything about me and he said he didn't. He said that her baby looked just like mine; in fact they could be twins. I told them that they almost are. They are by the same daddy, born on the same day, and look alike. That sounds like twins to me.

This information was hard to digest. Charlene and I were both pregnant at the same time by the same man and had our babies on the same day. Now what do I do with this information? Do I contact Charlene and update her? Should I wait until the paternity results are in and Ben is forced to pay child support?

I bet Brian would get a kick out of knowing that he had a niece from Charlene and by his ex-wife. That should really fuck with his head. So Karma has a sister named Evelyn. I hope that they get a chance to meet one day.

Charlene:

I was secretly hoping that Ava was in the mall with Lance, but she wasn't. I didn't ask about Ava, but I made sure I gave him all the details about what's been going on with me. I knew that it would get back to Ava. Although I didn't ask for information about Ava, Lance didn't offer up any information either.

When I got home, I put the baby to sleep. I checked my emails and had several. Most were advertisements, but one email caught my eye. It was from Ava. She said that she heard that I was a new mommy and so was she. She sent me pictures of her daughter Karma. I was shocked when I saw her. If it wasn't for the fact that I know that Evelyn hasn't been out of my sight since she was born, I would have thought that Ava kidnapped her and took these pictures. When I looked deeper, I noticed that Karma had lips like her mom and her eyes were light brown.

I replied to her email and sent her a picture of Evelyn. I congratulated her on being a brand-new mom also. I thought about asking her to meet up so that we could talk, but she beat me to it. Right after I sent the picture of Evelyn, she sent an email inviting me to brunch. I happily accepted.

Ava:

I reached out to Charlene via email. She accepted my invitation to brunch on Sunday after church. I didn't know how I was going to tell her, but I figured that Ben would keep it a secret forever if he could. I didn't want to ruin their marriage, but I wasn't going to hide Karma.

Ben surprised me. He didn't even fight me on the child support. He didn't even ask to see the baby; oh well, it's his loss and my gain. I get a healthy amount of money every two weeks from him. If I don't want to work, I won't have to. I guess the rape worked out in my favor after all.

When I met with Charlene, she had Evelyn with her. I had Karma with me too. She gave me a hug and we sat down to order some brunch. Charlene cut out all of the niceties and basically said that she knew Karma and Evelyn were sisters. She knew it as soon as she saw Karma's picture.

She asked me if I knew that she was seeing Ben. I told her that I didn't know Ben was seeing anyone at the time. I also told her about how Ben drugged me and raped me. I thought she was going to call me a liar, but she didn't. She actually cried for me. She said that she believed me and that Ben was too freaky for her taste. She wouldn't put it past him to take it if it wasn't offered to him. He was addicted to sex, plain and simple.

I told Charlene that he pays child support. She said that she knows. Just as I had Craig, she had a cousin that did private investigating. He got her all the information that she needed. I was impressed; I asked her if she was going to confront Ben. She said in time she would, but not yet. We decided that it was for the best that we keep in touch, but not to let Ben know. I agreed. I was just happy to have my friend back.

Ben:

As I was driving down the Blue Hill Avenue, I thought that I was seeing things. I thought I saw Ava and Charlene going into a breakfast spot together. Both of them had their babies. I had never seen Ava's kid; I just saw her in pictures that I had someone take of her without her knowing. Karma and Evelyn looked like they were the same baby. I got some strong ass genes.

I parked my car and waited for them to go their separate ways. I then followed Ava home. When she got to her house, I waited outside parked in my car for about a half of an hour. I then went into my trunk and pulled out a teddy bear that I was going to give to Evelyn. I put the teddy bear in the bag on top of the other gift that I had for Ava.

Surprisingly, the bitch opened the door for me. I walked in the place like I owned it. She saw the teddy bear and opened her mouth to thank me. I pulled the teddy bear out and threw it on the floor. She looked down at the floor and then stared back up with me with a look of confusion. By that time, I had already reached into my gift bag and splashed some battery acid in her face.

I've never heard a scream so painful before. It actually sent a chill through me. This bitch needed to be taught a lesson. I told her that the next time I saw her around Charlene and my child, I would have someone kill her faggot-ass friend that she loves so much. If that didn't keep her ass out of my business, I'd kill her mother.

I had to get out of there. She wouldn't stop screaming and neither would the baby. I thought about checking in on the baby and then changed my mind. She'd be okay. I only disfigured her mother. I didn't kill her. She could still tend to her crying baby. I don't know what she told Charlene, but I wasn't looking forward to the conversation waiting for me at home. If Ava cost me my life with Charlene and Evelyn, I don't know what I'd do. They are my life!

As I drive home, I think about how I could ever explain having a baby with Ava. It's not as if I can deny it. Both of my babies look like each other. I could lie and say that I got drunk one night and Ava threw herself on me. Ava was a freak and I'm sure Charlene knew that. Shit, I don't know what I'm going to say. It definitely won't be the truth.

Craig:

I found out what happened to my little cousin. The only thing to describe how she looks would be to compare her to that guy in that movie *Mask*. Her face was all jacked up. I really didn't know much about Ben Ford, but I made it my business to find out quick.

He had a few of the same connects that I had, but the ones that he had owed me big time. I decided to cash in on my favors. This time it was personal. Ben was going to die, but not before I kidnapped and tortured each member of his immediate family. Nobody would be excluded; I'm killing women and children. Yes, that means Charlene and her baby too. He has no idea who he is fucking with!

TO BE CONTINUED.....

43827418R00087

Made in the USA
Middletown, DE
20 May 2017